WITHDRAWN

W9-APO-275

SONIC:
GENESIS

IAN FLYNN
WRITER

PATRICK SPAZIANTE
PENCIL BREAK-DOWNS
PARTS I & II

TRACY YARDLEY!
PENCIL FINISHES
PARTS I & II
FULL PENCILS
PARTS III, IV & PROLOGUE

BEN BATES
FULL PENCILS - EPILOGUE

TERRY AUSTIN
INKS

MATT HERMS
COLORS

JOHN WORKMAN
LETTERS

COVER BY
PATRICK SPAZIANTE

PAUL KAMINSKI
EDITOR/EXEC. DIRECTOR
OF EDITORIAL

SPECIAL THANKS TO
ANTHONY GACCIONE, CINDY CHAU, and JUDY GILBERTSON AT SEGA LICENSING

ISBN: 978-1-936975-08-2

TABLE OF CONTENTS

PREVIOUSLY IN SONIC THE HEDGEHOG™

DR. IVO "EGGMAN" ROBOTNIK and his EGGMAN EMPIRE have threatened the freedom and happiness of everyone on the planet Mobius for as long as SONIC THE HEDGEHOG can remember! But it seems like things have gone from BAD to WORSE!

IT BEGAN WITH A BEATDOWN!

Sonic and Eggman fought what they thought was their final battle! Eggman's city had been reduced to ruin and only his **EGGDOME** bunker remained!

Sonic's victory drove Dr. Eggman to complete MADNESS! Our heroes had saved the world!

Or so they thought...

THEN CAME THE IRON DOMINION!

Led by shrewd technomancer THE IRON QUEEN, the IRON DOMINION took over the EggDome and the empire!

With a legion of ninjas, her partner THE IRON KING, and Eggman's own love-stricken nephew, SNIVELY, the IRON DOMINION conquered Sonic's city of New Mobotropolis!

Sonic, accompanied by SALLY, TAILS and MONKEY KHAN, led the heroes in their fight for freedom, traveling to the Dragon Kingdom to disrupt the Iron Queen's support from abroad!

EGGMAN: BACK FROM THE BRINK

In the chaos that ensued between the Freedom Fighters and the Iron Dominion, Dr. Eggman escaped! What was once a babbling, drooling shell of a man had "reasoned" his way back to sanity. Every failure, setback, and defeat -- all at the hands of Sonic -- suddenly made sense.

Taking Snively and "what was left" of his subordinate LIEN-DA, he snuck into the darkest corners of the EggDome and began to work in the shadows...

THE RETURN OF IXIS NAUGUS

With the IRON DOMINION defeated and EGGMAN in hiding, our heroes finally had a moment to rest! But that didn't last long! Sonic was betrayed by former ally GEOFFREY ST. JOHN, who revealed himself to be a sleeper agent of the evil wizard IXIS NAUGUS! Manipulating pop-star MINA MONGOOSE and agitating leftover stress from the Iron Dominion invasion, this new duo began sowing seeds of fear into the minds of New Mobotropolis's citizens, all in a carefully planned attempt at making Naugus king!

TERROR FROM TWO SIDES!

Sonic turned his attention inward to deal with the crisis at home. In doing so, he forgot about the Eggman... And now, "The Doctor is in!"

Since the fall of the IRON DOMINION, the doctor's cyborg army, THE DARK EGG LEGION, began constructing massive docking stations across the planet. But why? What was EGGMAN doing all this time? He has finished his greatest creation. With the BLUE CHAOS EMERALD powering its core, he has revealed the EggDome's true purpose!

What has been hiding in plain sight for over twenty-five issues launched with an earth-shattering force!

THE DEATH EGG HAS RETURNED.

MOMENTS AGO...
WOO!
...DEEP WITHIN THE DEATH EGG MARK 2.
HA HA HA! THAT'S IT, SONIC! YOU'RE PUTTING ON QUITE THE SHOW!
SONIC! IT'S JUST STALLING US! WE'VE GOT TO MOVE ON!

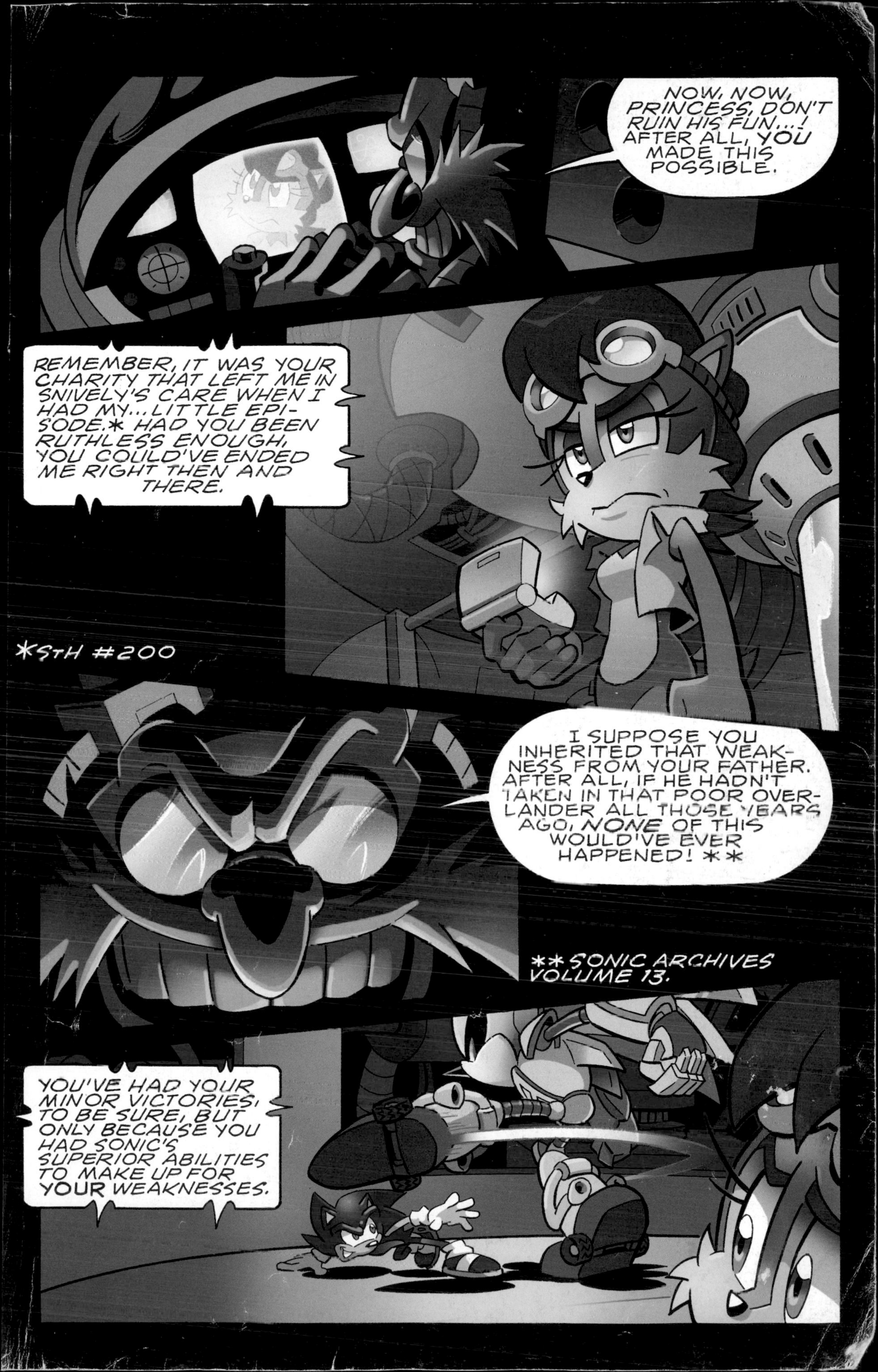
NOW, NOW, PRINCESS, DON'T RUIN HIS FUN...! AFTER ALL, YOU MADE THIS POSSIBLE.
REMEMBER, IT WAS YOUR CHARITY THAT LEFT ME IN SNIVELY'S CARE WHEN I HAD MY... LITTLE EPISODE.* HAD YOU BEEN RUTHLESS ENOUGH, YOU COULD'VE ENDED ME RIGHT THEN AND THERE.
*StH #200
I SUPPOSE YOU INHERITED THAT WEAKNESS FROM YOUR FATHER. AFTER ALL, IF HE HADN'T TAKEN IN THAT POOR OVERLANDER ALL THOSE YEARS AGO, NONE OF THIS WOULD'VE EVER HAPPENED! **
**SONIC ARCHIVES VOLUME 13.
YOU'VE HAD YOUR MINOR VICTORIES, TO BE SURE, BUT ONLY BECAUSE YOU HAD SONIC'S SUPERIOR ABILITIES TO MAKE UP FOR YOUR WEAKNESSES.

AND YOU-- ACK!
SIR, STAGE ONE IS FULLY CHARGED AND READY.
MARVELOUS!
TH-TH-THIS WILL AFFECT US ALL, YOU KNOW...
OH, GROW UP. YOU WON'T FEEL A THING.
IT'S BEEN FUN, CHILDREN. BUT THE WEAPON IS ARMED, AND I MUST GET TO FIRING IT. FAREWELL!
SONIC! WE'RE OUT OF TIME! WE'VE GOT TO MOVE!
SORRY, WHAT? JUST A SEC! I'M NOT DONE WITH "TINY" HERE.

I'M GOING AHEAD! NICOLE, CAN YOU TRACK WHERE HIS VOICE WAS COMING FROM?
VVVVRMMN
AH-AH! THAT'S FAR ENOUGH!
VVT
BLAM BLAM BLAM
SALLY!
GRNK!
BOOP

...SAL...?
SALLY!

SONIC: GENESIS

PART ONE

WELCOME TO A WHOLE NEW WORLD--ONE UNIQUE AND BEYOND WHAT YOU KNOW FROM THE SEGA GAMES!--WHERE WE BEGIN THE ALL-NEW, ALL-DIFFERENT ADVENTURES OF A SPEEDY BLUE HERO NAMED SONIC THE HEDGEHOG!
WHOA... FEELS LIKE I DOZED OFF FOR A MINUTE THERE...! WHAT WAS I DOING AGAIN?...
GENESIS
Part One: IN THE BEGINNING...
WRITER: IAN FLYNN
PENCIL BREAK-DOWNS: PATRICK SPAZIANTE
PENCIL FINISHES: TRACY YARDLEY!
INKS: TERRY AUSTIN
COLORS: MATT HERMS
LETTERS: JOHN WORKMAN
COVER BY PATRICK SPAZIANTE
EDITOR: PAUL KAMINSKI
EDITOR-IN-CHIEF: VICTOR GORELICK
PRESIDENT: MIKE PELLERITO
SPECIAL THANKS TO CINDY CHAU, JERRY CHU, AND JUDY GILBERTSON AT SEGA LICENSING

THAT'S RIGHT. DUDES ARE MISSING, AS WELL AS A TON OF ANIMALS...!
AND I'M JUST THE HEDGEHOG TO FIND OUT WHAT'S GOING ON!
I DON'T THINK EVERYONE DECIDED TO MIGRATE OR GO ON A VACA--
YOW! WHAT'S THAT?!
BESIDES UNFRIENDLY.

...AND NUMEROUS.
WHAT'S UP, GUYS?
OR IS IT GIRLS? DO ROBOTS GET GENDERS? HOW ABOUT A NAME--? I'LL CALL YOU GUYS...
...MOTOBUGS! WHICH SEEMS ...ODDLY APPROPRIATE.
LIKE... REALLY APPROPRIATE. *HUH.* I GUESS THIS SOLVES THE MYSTERY OF WHAT HAPPENED TO ALL THE ANIMALS, AT LEAST.

HEY, THERE.
SO...WHO BUILT YOU--
--AND WHY DID THEY THINK IT WAS COOL TO STUFF YOU FULL OF CRITTERS?
ALL RIGHT, BUDDY--MUSH! TAKE ME TO YOUR LEADER!
SOON...
AND WITH THAT, I'VE REACHED QUOTA.
UNCLE WILL BE SO PLEASED WITH--
--MEEK?!

WHAT--
--HOW--
--WHY?!
THE NAME'S "SONIC THE HEDGEHOG."
I RESPOND BETTER TO "WHO," BUT I'M FLEXIBLE.
ARE YOU THE GUY BEHIND ALL THIS?
ONLY IN PART. I AM SNIVELY, LOWLY SERVANT TO A GRANDER DESIGN.
THE DESIGNS OF MY BRILLIANT UNCLE, DR. EGGMAN! HE WILL BRING ORDER TO THESE WILD LANDS! ALL GREENERY WILL BE PAVED! ALL FILTHY ANIMALS WILL POWER SHINY ROBOTS! THE WORLD WILL NOT ONLY WORK LIKE... BUT *BECOME* A WELL-OILED MACHINE!
WOW. WHAT A JERK.
HE'S BRILLIANT! BRILLIANT, I SAY!
NO, HE'S NOT!

WHOA! NEAT TRICK!
BAH! AS IF YOU COULD UNDERSTAND, YOU SMELLY ANIMAL!
I'VE GOT A FEW SURPRISES MYSELF!
H-HOW DID HE MOVE...
...THAT FAST?
FOR EXAMPLE...
GAH!
OVER HERE, NEEDLE-NOSE!
YOU FREAK OF NATURE--!

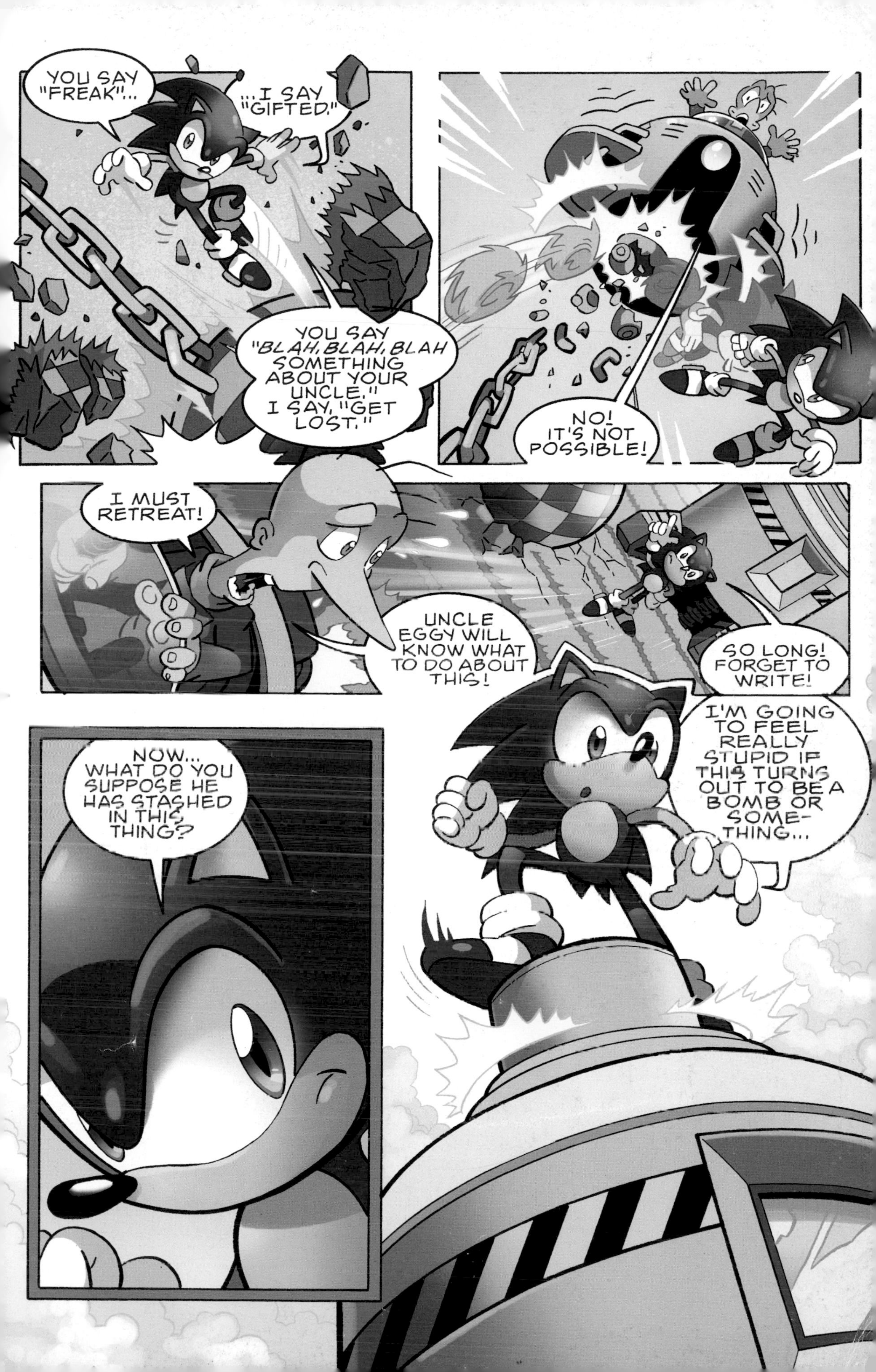
YOU SAY "FREAK"...
...I SAY "GIFTED."
YOU SAY "BLAH, BLAH, BLAH SOMETHING ABOUT YOUR UNCLE." I SAY, "GET LOST."
NO! IT'S NOT POSSIBLE!
I MUST RETREAT!
UNCLE EGGY WILL KNOW WHAT TO DO ABOUT THIS!
SO LONG! FORGET TO WRITE!
NOW... WHAT DO YOU SUPPOSE HE HAS STASHED IN THIS THING?
I'M GOING TO FEEL REALLY STUPID IF THIS TURNS OUT TO BE A BOMB OR SOME-THING...

GAK! DOES EVERY-THING THIS EGGMAN GUY BUILDS EXPLODE ?!
OH... UM... WOW.
HELLO!
YOU...YOU MUST BE...
...OUR RESCUER.
SONIC THE HEDGEHOG. YOU'RE SOME OF THE FOLKS THAT WENT MISSING, RIGHT?
THAT'S RIGHT. MY NAME IS SALLY ACORN. THESE ARE MY FRIENDS, BOOMER WALRUS AND ANTOINE DEPARDIEU.
HEYA!
IS ZE HORRIBLE TINY MAN GONE?

NICE TO MEET YOU. NOW IF YOU'LL EXCUSE ME, I'VE GOT MORE 'BOTS TO BASH!
NO! WAIT, PLEASE!
MAKE IT QUICK. NOBODY WILL BE RESCUING THEM-SELVES.
MY FRIENDS AND I ARE TRYING TO GET TO THE SOURCE OF THE PROBLEM. WE WANT TO STOP THE MADMAN BEHIND THESE KIDNAPPINGS.
AND WHAT'S WORSE, WE THINK THE SAME GUY IS BEHIND ALL THE BIG EARTHQUAKES WE'VE HAD LATELY.
DR. EGGMAN IS RAVAGING THE LAND AND TERRORIZING THE PEOPLE.
WE'RE DEDICATED TO FIGHTING FOR OUR FREEDOM...
AND I--WE--COULD REALLY USE SOMEONE LIKE YOU.
I DUNNO...YOU GUYS MIGHT SLOW ME DOWN!
WE'VE ALREADY SCOUTED A WAY TO HIS STRONGHOLD.
NOTHING'S QUICKER THAN A DIRECT ROUTE.
THEN BY ALL MEANS...
...LEAD THE WAY!
WOULD YOU KNOCK IT OFF?
I AM JUST WANTING TO BE SURE ZE COASTING IS CLEAR!

LATER...
...AND WE'RE PRETTY SURE THAT THERE'S SOME KIND OF UNDERGROUND PASSAGE THAT RUNS FROM THE MARBLE ZONE TO DR. EGGMAN'S LAIR.
I'LL ADMIT I HAD MY DOUBTS, BUT WE'RE DEFINITELY ON THE RIGHT TRACK NOW.
WHAT CHANGED YOUR MIND?
THE KILLER ROBOTS.
EEP!
CAREFUL, SONIC! THIS MODEL IS CALLED--
A CATER-KILLER!
OH, YOU'VE ...DONE RESEARCH YOURSELF?
...NO. IT JUST KIND OF... CAME TO ME.

AND THAT'S WHY THEY CALL YOU "BOOMER," RIGHT?
ALWAYS HAPPY TO HELP.
HERE COME MORE, BOYS!
I WOULD JUST BE GETTING IN ZE WAY. I SHALL WAIT OVER HERE, OKAY? OKAY!
THERE ...NICE AND SAFE.

EEEEEEK!
AIDEZ-MOI!
BATS!
HELP!!!
IL Y A DES
CHAUVES-
SOURIS!

WELL, THAT WAS MODERATELY ENTERTAINING...
THANK YOU, ANTOINE!
ANTOINE?!
WAY TO GO!
WE NEVER WOULD'VE SEEN THAT AMBUSH COMING!
AH, WELL, AHOO-HOO-HOO! I DO WHAT I CAN...

YEAH, RIGHT.
HE MEANT TO DO THAT, MY SPINY BLUE...
YO, BOOMER!
WHAT ARE YOU DOING?
WE JUST GOT DONE SMASHING THOSE.
I'M REPRO-GRAMMING IT.
HOW COOL WOULD IT BE TO HAVE ONE ON OUR SIDE?

PRETTY COOL, I GUESS.
THE PROBLEM, THOUGH...
...IS WE WOULD NEED AN ANIMAL TO POWER IT.
I DON'T WANT TO STOOP...
...TO EGGMAN'S LEVEL.
MAYBE WE WON'T HAVE TO...
EXCUSE ME? COULD WE ASK A FAVOR OF YOU?
WOULD YOU RIDE INSIDE THE ROBOT FOR JUST A LITTLE WHILE? IT WOULD REALLY HELP US OUT.
SHE'S AGREED TO HELP US.
THANKS, LITTLE FLICKY!
IN YOU GO!

OKAY, THAT'S PRETTY COOL.
THINK YOU CAN KEEP UP WITH ME?
THEN LET'S CLEAR THE ROAD!

...WOW! LOOK AT THEM GO!
HA-HA! WAIT! FOR US!
EEEEEK!
ANOTHER EARTHQUAKE! BRACE YOUR-SELVES!
IT EXPOSED A MAGMA DEPOSIT! RUN!
ER... WHERE TO, SALLY?
SINKING! WE ARE SINKING!
WOW! THAT WAS WORSE THAN ANY OF THE LAST...
SONIC!!!

HANG ON, GUYS!
HANG ON TO THE BUZZ-BOMBER, BOYS!
OKAY, YOU WON ME OVER, BOOMER!
THAT THING'S PRETTY COOL FOR SURE!
IS IT HOT OUT HERE, OR IS IT JUST YOU?
S-SONIC! THIS IS HARDLY THE TIME OR PLACE...

YEAH, YOU'RE RIGHT. SOMETIMES I MOVE TOO FAST.
N-WELL, MAYBE, I MEAN...
THANKS FOR THE LIFT!
PLEASE TO BE ZE END OF ZE TERROR?
THE TERRORIZING HAS JUST BEGUN!
MYAH HA HA HA HA!
ZUT ALORS!
LOOKING AT YOUR OH-SO-ROUND SHAPE, I GUESS YOU'RE THIS "EGGMAN" GUY EVERYONE'S TALKING ABOUT?
INDEED...
AND YOU MUST BE SONIC, THE NASTY LITTLE BOY WHO BULLIED MY NEPHEW THIS MORNING.
YEP. I CAN'T WAIT TO DO THE SAME TO YOU.
OH-HO-HO-HO! WE WILL SEE ABOUT THAT!

SONIC!
WOW. LOOK AT THEM GO!
THERE'S NOBODY ELSE LIKE THEM!
YEAH!...
"...SO WHY DOES ALL THIS SEEM SO FAMILIAR?"
MY! YOU'RE A QUICK ONE!
FASTER THAN FAST, DOC!
AND SWIFTER THAN SW-- OOPS! THAT'S NOT GOOD.
NO. NOT GOOD AT ALL. GAME OVER, RODENT.

BAH! WHAT DO YOU THINK YOU'RE DOING ?!
TAKE THAT, YOU TRAITOR! HA! HA HA HA HA--
--HA?
NOOOOO!!!

THAT TEARS IT! NO MORE TOYING AROUND WITH YOU!
ONCE MY MASTER PLAN IS COMPLETE, YOU WILL ALL SUFFER MY WRATH!
...JUST AS SOON AS I FIGURE OUT WHAT THAT PLAN IS. JUST WHAT IS THAT GLORIOUS BATTLE-STATION FOR...?
YO, SAL! TELL THAT FLICKY I OWE IT ONE!
YOU WERE VERY BRAVE.
THANK YOU SO VERY MUCH!

WELL, THAT WAS FUN. WHAT'S NEXT?
SERIOUSLY?! YOU'RE AMAZING!
I KNOW, I KNOW.
I'M *SURE* YOU DO.

THAT SHOULD BE THE WAY INTO THE UNDERGROUND PASSAGE.
HOW DOES IT LOOK, ANTOINE?
UM... PERILOUS?

WELCOME TO THE *BEGINNING* OF A *WHOLE NEW ADVENTURE!* WHAT *NEW PERILS* WILL OUR HEROES FIND IN THIS *NEW WORLD?*

DON'T MISS EVEN *MORE* ADVENTURES IN *SONIC UNIVERSE*, *THE SONIC ARCHIVES*, AND THE *SONIC SELECTS*!

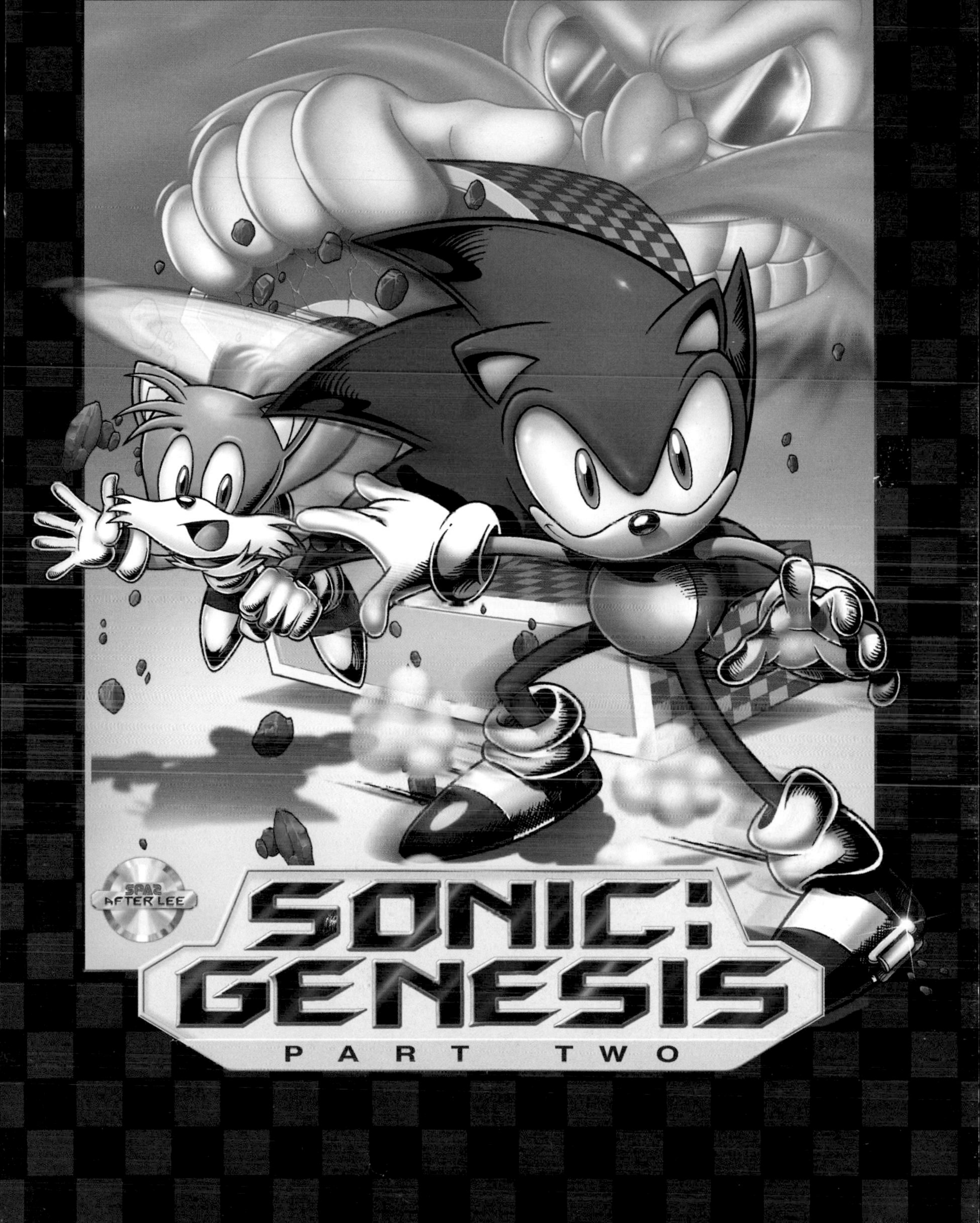
SPAZ
AFTER LEE
SONIC:
GENESIS
PART TWO

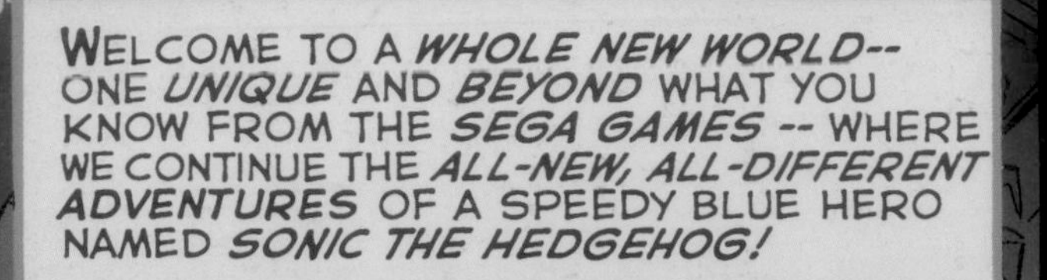

GENESIS

Part Two: FRIENDS AND FATE

WRITER: IAN FLYNN
PENCIL BREAKDOWNS: PATRICK "SPAZ" SPAZIANTE
PENCIL FINISHES: TRACY YARDLEY!
INKS: TERRY AUSTIN
COLORS: MATT HERMS
LETTERS: JOHN WORKMAN

COVER BY PATRICK SPAZIANTE • EDITOR: PAUL KAMINSKI
EDITOR-IN-CHIEF: VICTOR GORELICK • PRESIDENT: MIKE PELLERITO
SPECIAL THANKS TO CINDY CHAU AND JUDY GILBERTSON AT SEGA LICENSING

SONIC THE HEDGEHOG
SUPER-SPEEDY HERO

SALLY ACORN
COURAGEOUS LEADER

BOOMER WALRUS
MECHANIC

ANTOINE DEPARDIEU
EASILY STARTLED

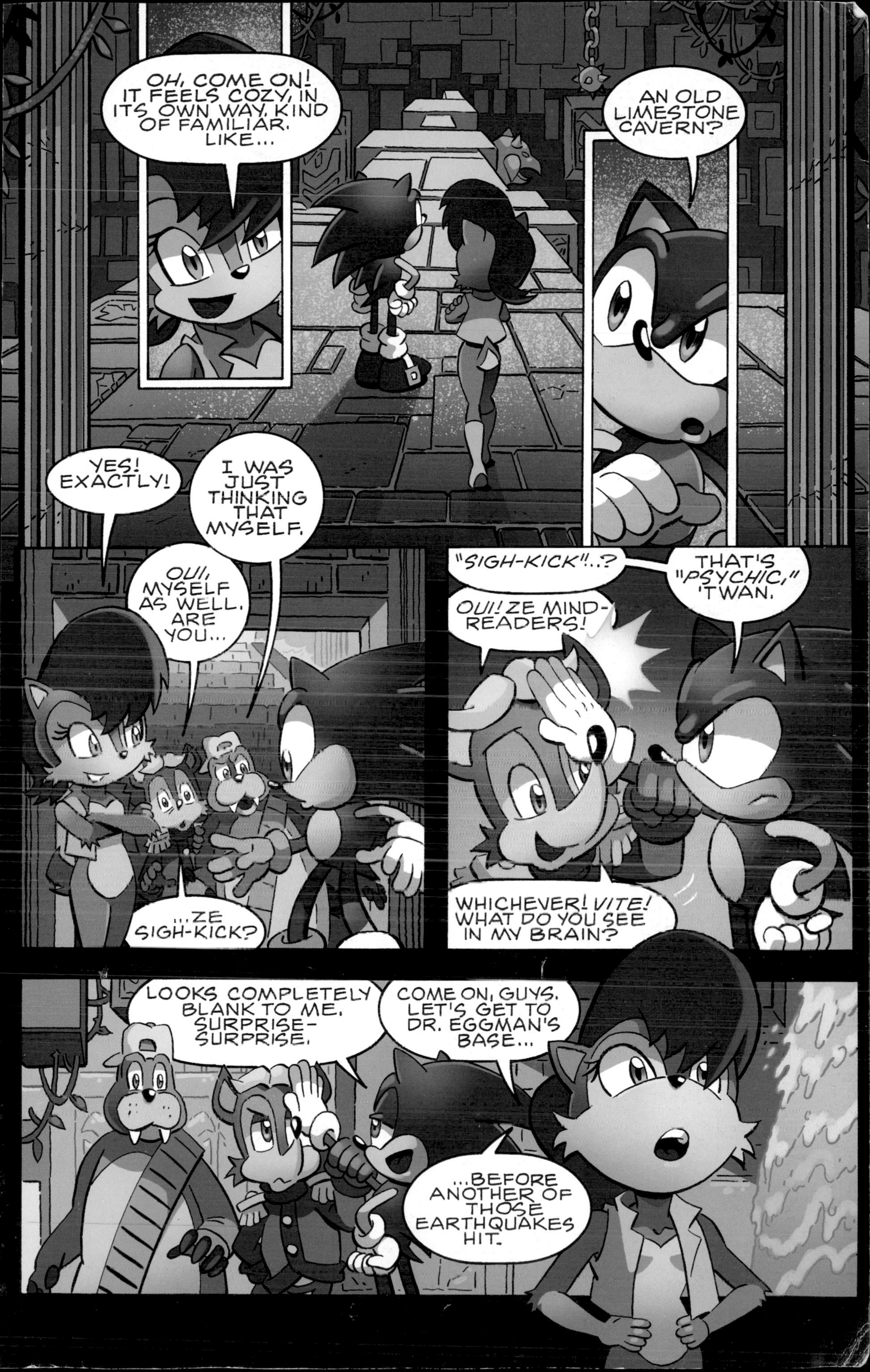
OH, COME ON! IT FEELS COZY, IN ITS OWN WAY. KIND OF FAMILIAR. LIKE...
AN OLD LIMESTONE CAVERN?
YES! EXACTLY!
I WAS JUST THINKING THAT MYSELF.
OUI, MYSELF AS WELL. ARE YOU...
...ZE SIGH-KICK?
"SIGH-KICK"..?
THAT'S "PSYCHIC," 'TWAN.
OUI! ZE MIND-READERS!
WHICHEVER! VITE! WHAT DO YOU SEE IN MY BRAIN?
LOOKS COMPLETELY BLANK TO ME. SURPRISE-SURPRISE.
COME ON, GUYS. LET'S GET TO DR. EGGMAN'S BASE...
...BEFORE ANOTHER OF THOSE EARTHQUAKES HIT.

THAT WAS PRETTY SLICK HOW YOU USED THAT ROBOT TO HELP US EARLIER.* WHERE DID YOU LEARN THAT STUFF?
AH, WELL. I DUNNO. IT JUST COMES NATURALLY TO ME.
*SEE LAST ISSUE!
WELL, IT SURE CAME IN HANDY! YO, SAL, I'LL GIVE YOU A--
ALLOW ME, MA CHÉRIE!
THANKS, SWEETIE!
"MA CHERIE" ...?
"SWEETIE" ...?!

HEY, SAL? JUST HOW LONG HAVE YOU AND...
HOW LONG HAVE I WHAT? SONIC? HELLO?
...OOOKAY, C'MON, WE'LL DIVE TO THE NEXT PART OF THE--
DIVE?! INTO THE WATER?
UNLESS YOU PLAN TO DIVE INTO SOLID ROCK...?

NO WORRIES! RUINS LIKE THESE ARE FULL OF AIR POCKETS! WE'LL BE FINE!...
YEAH, BUT ...I CAN'T SWIM.
LIKE... AT ALL.
DON'T WORRY. YOU'LL DO JUST FINE WITH ME.
...SURE.
LEAD THE WAY.
OKAY... THIS ISN'T SO BAD...

!
GREAT. NOW WHAT?
OF COURSE...
...THERE WOULD BE ROBOTS DOWN HERE.
HERO TIME!
...IF I COULD, Y'KNOW, GET SOME SPEED GOING.
I HATE WATER.

IF I DODGE, I'LL LOSE ALL MY MOMENTUM.
AND NOW THAT I'VE GOT SPEED --THERE IS THIS!
UNLESS...

HRRRGH...!
ANTOINE ...!
REACH!
RUMBLE
EARTH-QUAKE!
ANTOINE!
WHOA!
SONIC!

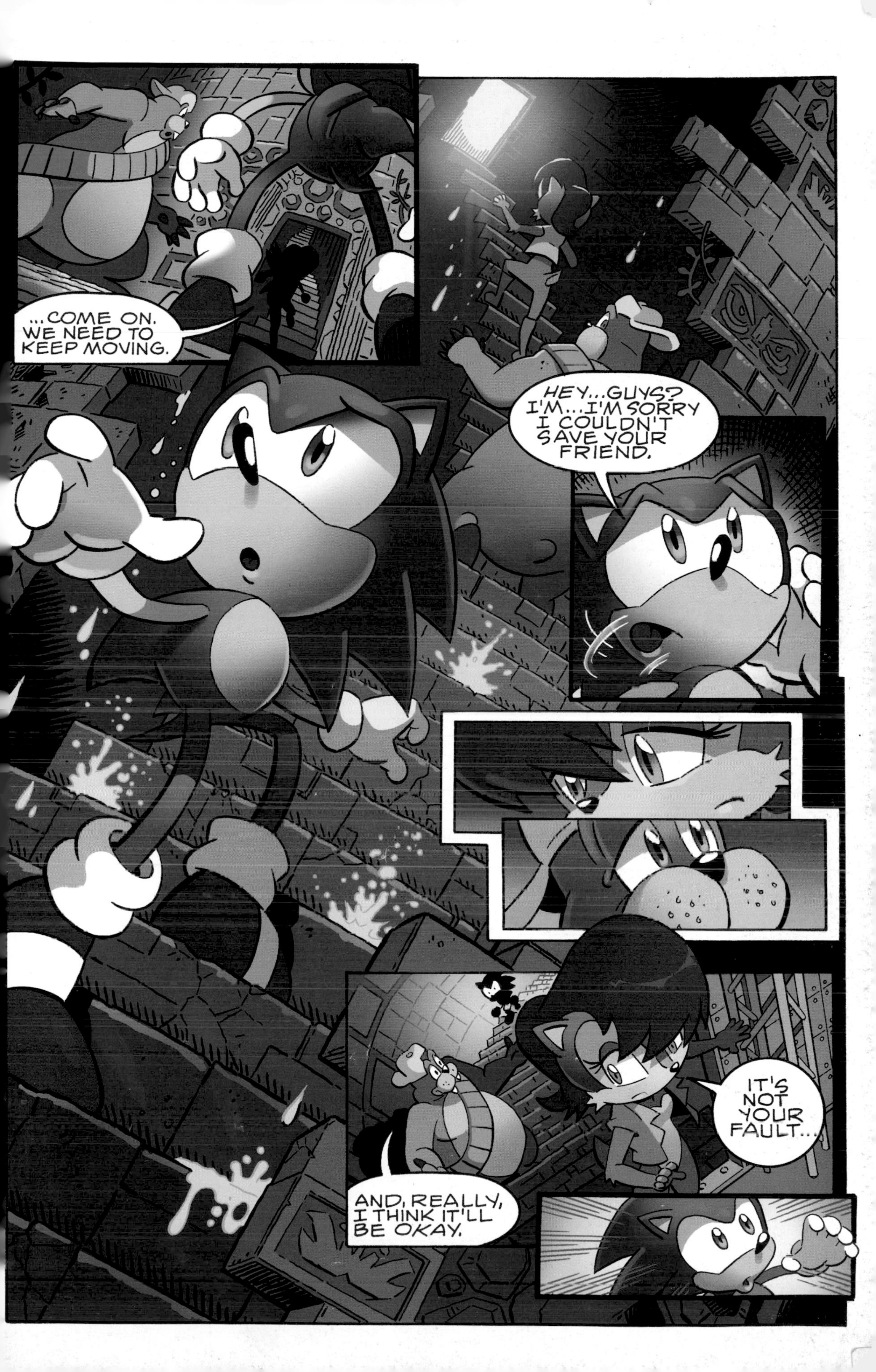
...COME ON. WE NEED TO KEEP MOVING.
HEY...GUYS? I'M...I'M SORRY I COULDN'T SAVE YOUR FRIEND.
IT'S NOT YOUR FAULT...
AND, REALLY, I THINK IT'LL BE OKAY.

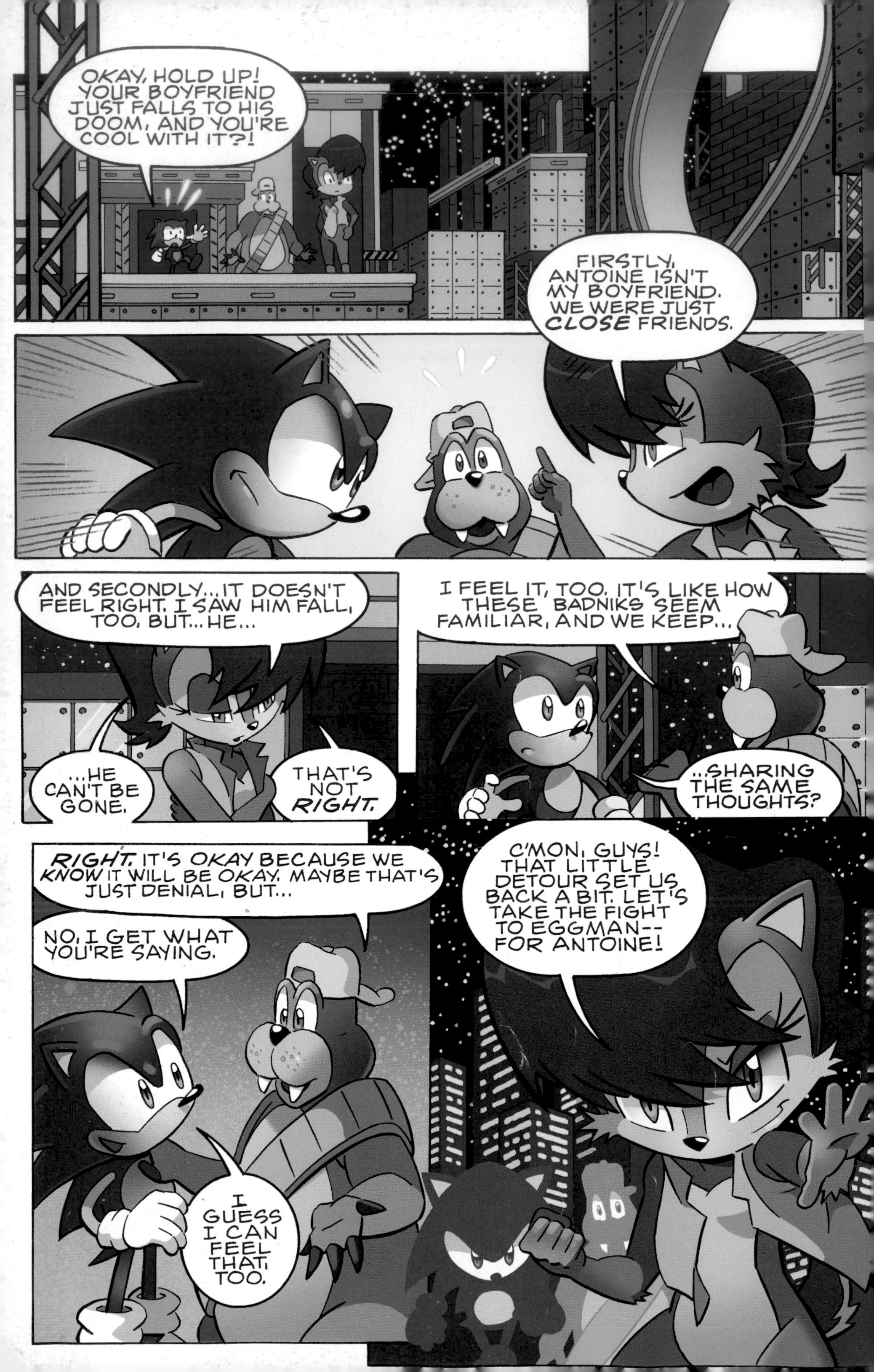
OKAY, HOLD UP! YOUR BOYFRIEND JUST FALLS TO HIS DOOM, AND YOU'RE COOL WITH IT?!
FIRSTLY, ANTOINE ISN'T MY BOYFRIEND. WE WERE JUST CLOSE FRIENDS.
AND SECONDLY... IT DOESN'T FEEL RIGHT. I SAW HIM FALL, TOO, BUT... HE...
...HE CAN'T BE GONE.
THAT'S NOT RIGHT.
I FEEL IT, TOO. IT'S LIKE HOW THESE BADNIKS SEEM FAMILIAR, AND WE KEEP...
...SHARING THE SAME THOUGHTS?
RIGHT. IT'S OKAY BECAUSE WE KNOW IT WILL BE OKAY. MAYBE THAT'S JUST DENIAL, BUT...
NO, I GET WHAT YOU'RE SAYING.
I GUESS I CAN FEEL THAT, TOO.
C'MON, GUYS! THAT LITTLE DETOUR SET US BACK A BIT. LET'S TAKE THE FIGHT TO EGGMAN-- FOR ANTOINE!

WELL... HERE WE ARE. WELCOME TO THE SCENIC SCRAP BRAIN ZONE.
SERIOUSLY?
"SCRAP BRAIN"?
WHAT DOES THAT EVEN MEAN?
WHAT DO YOU WANT, SONIC? HE'S A MADMAN WHO PUTS ANIMALS INTO ROBOTS AND WANTS TO CONQUER THE WORLD.
AND LOOKS LIKE A TALKING EGG TO BOOT. NAH, THIS PLACE NEEDS A COOLER NAME, LIKE...LIKE... "ROBOTROPOLIS."
OOH-YEAH! OR-OR-OR... HOW ABOUT "NEW MEGA-OPOLIS"?
NAH, YOU'RE TRYING TOO HARD, BUDDY.
I GUESS. "ROBOTROPOLIS" DOES HAVE A RING TO IT.

IT'S TOO QUIET.
DOCTOR EGGMAN KNOWS WE'RE COMING. I WAS EXPECTING MORE...
...TRAPS?!
RRGH!
SONIC!
SALLY!

NO!
NOT AGAIN!
HRNH! WHEN THIS IS OVER...
...YOU'RE LAYING OFF JOE'S SUSHI!
I'LL GO ON AN EVERY-THING DIET! JUST DON'T DROP ME!
BOOMER, I'M SLIPPING! IS THERE ANY-THING...
...YOU CAN BRACE ON?

NOTHING! DROP ME AND SAVE YOUR-SELF!
NO, YOU'RE NOT PUTTING ME THROUGH THAT AGAIN!
PULL, MAN! *PULL!*

QUICK, PEOPLE! GET BELOW BEFORE ANYTHING ELSE HAPPENS!
YOU DO HAVE SOME KIND OF MAP OF THIS PLACE, RIGHT?
SORRY, SONIC. I'M FLYING BLIND HERE.
EVEN IF I DID, I DOUBT THIS PLACE WOULD MAKE ANY SENSE.
WOW. BET HE NEVER HAS TO LOOK FOR A CAN OPENER.

NOW...IF I WAS A MAD SCIENTIST IN HIDING, WHERE WOULD I--

--BE?

RIGHT HERE, YOU MISERABLE RODENT! YOU'VE DONE WELL TO GET THIS FAR.
THANKS...
...EGG-MAN.
I HAVE A REAL NAME, YOU KNOW!
I *HATE* THAT NICKNAME! WHY DOES EVERYONE CALL ME THAT?
LOOK, HOW ABOUT YOU SAVE US ALL A HEADACHE AND LET ME OUT OF THIS FORCE FIELD?
AH, BUT WHERE WOULD THE FUN BE IN THAT?
"FUN," HE SAYS...

AW, MAN--DEAD END!

MARVELOUS CHOICE OF WORDS! FAREWELL, BOY.

CREEEAK
EH? THAT SOUNDS LIKE THE--

--HYDRAULICS PIPE.

ANTOINE?! YOU'RE OKAY!
NON! I AM NOT ZE OKAY!
I WASH AROUND IN ZE DARK FOR HOURS! I AM DIZZY AND SOGGY AND FRIGHTENED AND...
...BONJOUR.
EEEEEEEEEE EEEEEEEEEEEE EEEEEEEEEK!
THANKS FOR THE SAVE, 'TWAN!

NOW I'VE GOT YOU-- HEY!
STAY AWAY!

GOT IT!
GOOD WORK! SORRY TO MAKE YOU WAIT, SONIC...!
EH, YOU WERE HERE IN SPIRIT.

YOU'RE-- NOT--
--GETTING --AWAY-- THAT-- EASILY!
HE ESCAPED... HKRRRRGH!... DOWN HERE...
...AND SEALED IT SHUT!

HEY! GET BACK HERE, YOU COWARD!
EGAD!
WOW-- YOU'RE PRETTY FAST FOR A FAT MAN!
YOU'LL PAY FOR THIS, RODENT!
NOT LIKELY!
AUGH!
AAAARGH! I HATE THAT HEDGEHOG!!!

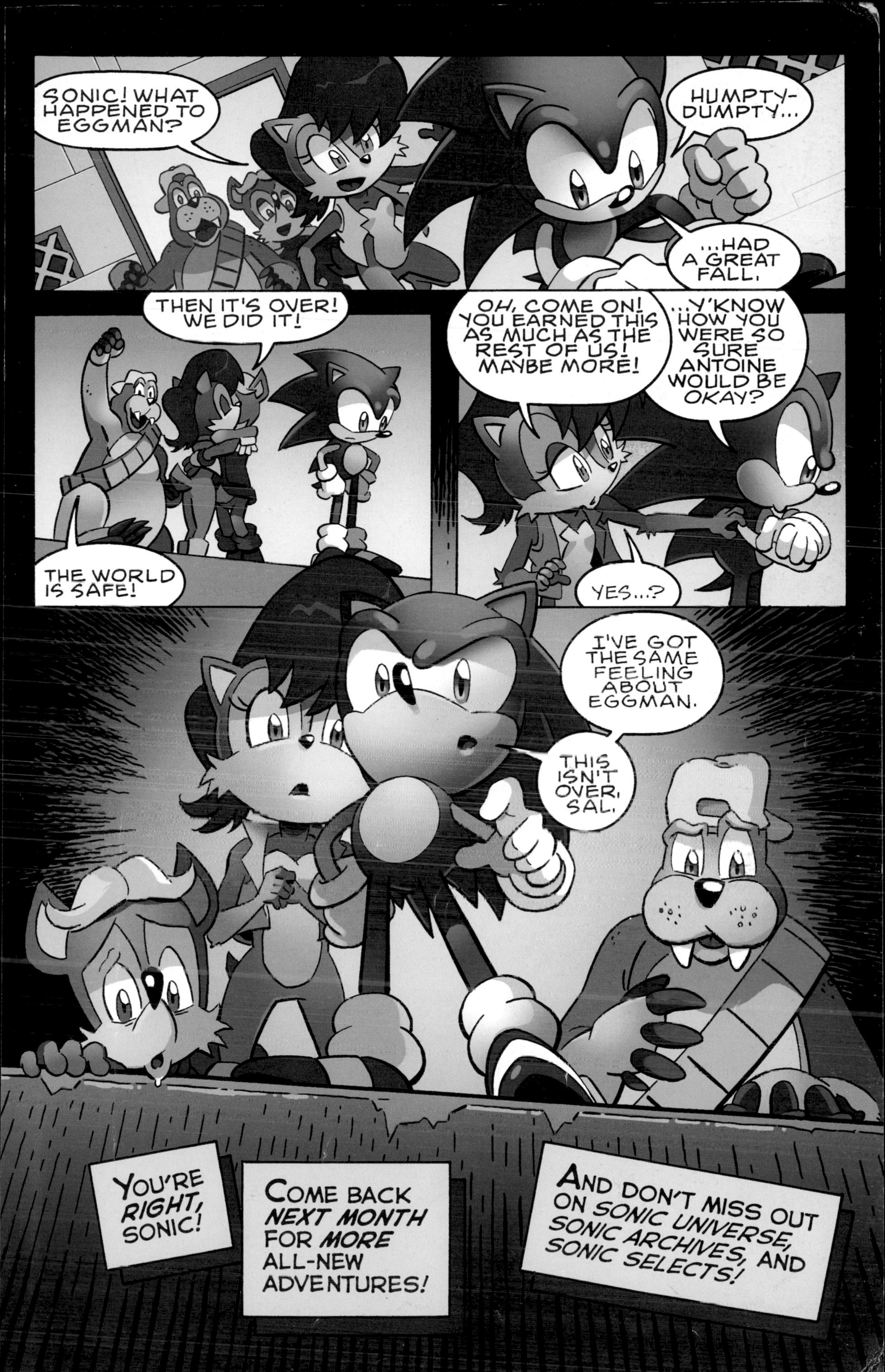
SONIC! WHAT HAPPENED TO EGGMAN?
HUMPTY-DUMPTY...
...HAD A GREAT FALL.
THEN IT'S OVER! WE DID IT!
THE WORLD IS SAFE!
OH, COME ON! YOU EARNED THIS AS MUCH AS THE REST OF US! MAYBE MORE!
...Y'KNOW HOW YOU WERE SO SURE ANTOINE WOULD BE OKAY?
YES...?
I'VE GOT THE SAME FEELING ABOUT EGGMAN.
THIS ISN'T OVER, SAL.
YOU'RE RIGHT, SONIC!
COME BACK NEXT MONTH FOR MORE ALL-NEW ADVENTURES!
AND DON'T MISS OUT ON SONIC UNIVERSE, SONIC ARCHIVES, AND SONIC SELECTS!

SONIC GENESIS

PART THREE

TAKE A GLIMPSE AT A WHOLE NEW WORLD-- ONE DIFFERENT FROM WHAT YOU KNOW FROM THE SEGA GAMES AND THE COMICS! -- WHERE WE ENTER THE EVER-CHANGING ADVENTURES OF A SPEEDY BLUE HERO NAMED SONIC THE HEDGEHOG!
GENESIS
Part Three: DIVIDE AND CONQUER
WRITER: IAN FLYNN
PENCILS: TRACY YARDLEY!
INKS: TERRY AUSTIN
COLORS: MATT HERMS
LETTERS: JOHN WORKMAN
COVER BY PATRICK "SPAZ" SPAZIANTE
EDITOR: PAUL KAMINSKI
EDITOR-IN-CHIEF: VICTOR GORELICK · PRESIDENT: MIKE PELLERITO
SPECIAL THANKS TO CINDY CHAU AND JUDY GILBERTSON AT SEGA LICENSING
YO, TAILS! WHAT'S UP?
SONIC!
ANTOINE DEPARDIEU
JUMPS AT SHADOWS
BOOMER WALRUS
BUDDING MECHANIC
DR. EGGMAN & SNIVELY
THE BAD GUYS!
SONIC THE HEDGEHOG
SPEEDY HERO
SALLY ACORN
COURAGEOUS LEADER

WHO ARE YOUR FRIENDS?
THESE DUDES HELPED ME OUT ON MY LAST ADVENTURE. WAIT UNTIL YOU HEAR ABOUT IT!
GUYS, THIS IS WHO I WAS TELLING YOU ABOUT. MILES PROWER IS THE SMARTEST KID I KNOW.
HI THERE! MY NAME IS SALLY.
H-HI, YOU CAN CALL ME "TAILS."
BONJOUR.
YOU'VE GOT AN F 1 WITH A 9B NINE-CYLINDER ROTARY ENGINE!
YEAH! IT'S SONIC'S, BUT HE LETS ME TAKE CARE OF IT FOR HIM!
AND YOU SHOULD GET ALONG GREAT WITH... UH... BOOMER?!
WHERE DID HE GO?
OH, MAN!

WAITAMINUTE! YOU ADDED A HIGH-BYPASS TURBOFAN ENGINE?!
WELL, SONIC DOES PREFER TO GO FAST. AND IT WASN'T TOO HARD TO CONNECT THE FUEL LINES...
AND YOU'RE *HOW* OLD?!
TOTALLY CALLED IT. THEY'LL BE LIKE THIS FOR *HOURS*.
IT'S CUTE!
BESIDES, WE COULD ALL USE SOMETHING TO BE CHEERFUL ABOUT.
I SAW YOU WORKING ON THAT COMPUTER BEFORE WE LEFT THE SCRAP BRAIN ZONE. NOTHING BUT BAD NEWS?
PRETTY MUCH.
DOCTOR EGGMAN'S PRODUCTION PLANTS ARE STILL RUNNING, AND IT LOOKS LIKE YOU WERE RIGHT-- HE DID SURVIVE.
AND THERE WERE NO LEADS ABOUT ALL THE RECENT--
RRRRRRUMBLLE!

THAT WAS THE WORST TREMOR YET. IF EGG-MAN IS BEHIND THEM, WE NEED TO STOP HIM BEFORE THE ENTIRE PLANET SHAKES APART!
WHICH WOULD STINK, 'CAUSE THAT'S WHERE I KEEP ALL MY STUFF.
SO LET'S CUT TO THE CHASE, FIND THE DOC, AND BEAT THE UGLY OFF HIM, WHICH MIGHT TAKE A WEEK, BUT HEY...
NO...
WE NEED TO DISMANTLE HIS INFRASTRUC-TURE FIRST. HIS SUPPORT LINES MUST BE CUT!
BUT THAT PLAN SOUNDS SO SLOW...
ARE YOU GOING ON ANOTHER ADVENTURE, SONIC? CAN I COME, TOO?
I DON'T KNOW... YOU'RE AWFULLY YOUNG...
DON'T WORRY ABOUT TAILS. I TAUGHT HIM HOW TO HANDLE HIM-SELF.
ENOUGH WAITING! WE'LL FOLLOW YOUR PLAN FOR NOW, SAL. YOU'VE GOT THE DIREC-TIONS TO EGG-MAN'S NEXT FACTORY?
I SURE DO! HE WON'T KNOW WHAT HIT HIM!

MEANWHILE...
WAHA-HA-HA! WITH PHASE ONE WELL BEHIND US, THIS GLORIOUS FLYING FORTRESS CAN MOVE ON TO PHASE TWO OF MY BRILLIANT PLAN!
ABOUT THAT, SIR. WHAT WAS PHASE ONE?
IT WAS BRILLIANT! WE DID THAT... THING...TO THE PLANET!
YOU KNOW...THAT THING...IT PRIMED MOBIUS FOR... PHASE TWO.
BAH! IT DOESN'T MATTER WHETHER YOU REMEMBER IT OR NOT!
WHATEVER IT WAS, IT SEVERELY DRAINED THE POWER RESERVES!

YES, BUT YOU DON'T HAVE TO WORRY ABOUT REFUELING FROM ALL YOUR FACTORIES AND BASES NOW! THE SEVEN CHAOS EMERALDS WE FOUND ARE RECHARGING THE STATION INCREDIBLY FAST!

YESSSS. ONCE FULLY POWERED, I WILL BE ABLE TO ROBOTIZE ALL OF MOBIUS IN ONE SHOT!

SINCE ALL WE HAVE TO DO IS WAIT FOR TOTAL VICTORY...
...I HAVE PLENTY OF TIME TO WORK ON THIS LITTLE "CHAOS IN THE EQUATION" LOGIC PUZZLE.
SIR?

THE UNPREDICTABLE, SNIVELY, THE QUANTUM VARIANT. THE UNEXPLAINABLE HICCUP IN THE SOUNDEST OF PLANS. THE HEDGEHOG...
H-HEDGE-HOG...?

ERM... SHOULDN'T WE BE PAYING SOME ATTENTION TO THE DIMENSIONAL DISTURBANCES? THEY'VE CAUSED HEAVY SEISMIC ACTIVITY RECENTLY...
...BUT PRELIMINARY READINGS SUGGEST A TOTAL SPACE-TIME COLLAPSE. IT'S LIKE REALITY HAS BEEN STRETCHED AND IS FIGHTING TO SNAP BACK.
HMM?
WHATEVER. I'LL HAVE WON BEFORE THEN.
LET ME WORK.
WHAT ABOUT THE REBEL MOBIANS WHO ATTACKED US? THEY'RE SURE TO TRY TO CAUSE MORE PROBLEMS!
OH, DON'T WORRY ABOUT THEM, SNIVELY.
I MADE SURE MY FACILITIES ARE READY...
...FOR UNINVITED GUESTS.

HERE WE ARE, FOLKS. THE CHEMICAL PLANT ZONE.
SOMEHOW I DON'T THINK THIS PLACE MEETS OCCUPATIONAL HAZARD GUIDELINES.
WHICH MEANS IT WILL BE A *LOT* OF FUN TO RUN AROUND IN!
IS HE POLLUTING FOR POLLUTION'S SAKE? WHY WOULD HE NEED TO PRODUCE THIS MUCH CHEMICAL FUEL?
UNLESS HE'S STOCKPILING IT ALL...
OR IF IT'S MEANT FOR A TRULY *MONSTROUS* MACHINE!
CAN YOU IMAGINE HOW MANY JOULES THAT MUCH FUEL COULD PRODUCE?!
CAN YOU IMAGINE A DEVICE THAT *NEEDED* THAT KIND OF POWER?!
ARE WE TRYING TO STOP ZE MADMAN'S SCHEMES, OR ARE WE PUTTING TOGETHER ZE FANNING CLUB FOR HIM?
DON'T BE SUCH A SPOIL-SPORT, ANTOINE. C'MON, LET'S SEE ABOUT SHUTTING THIS PLACE DOWN.

WOW. THIS PLACE IS DECEPTIVELY HUGE!
I WAS KNOWING IT! WE ARE TRAPPED IN HERE FOREVER!
GIVE IT A REST, 'TWAN. WE CAN FIND OUR WAY OUT EASILY.
THE REAL PROBLEM IS FINDING THE WAY WE WANT TO GO.
ALL THESE PIPES HAVE TO GO SOMEWHERE, RIGHT? I'LL JUST SPEED THROUGH THEM AND FIND WHERE WE NEED TO GO!
I'M SURE I CAN FIGURE OUT WHICH PIPE WE NEED TO FOLLOW, AND...
YEAH-YEAH-YEAH! RACE YA!
HA HA HA! YOU'RE CRAZY!

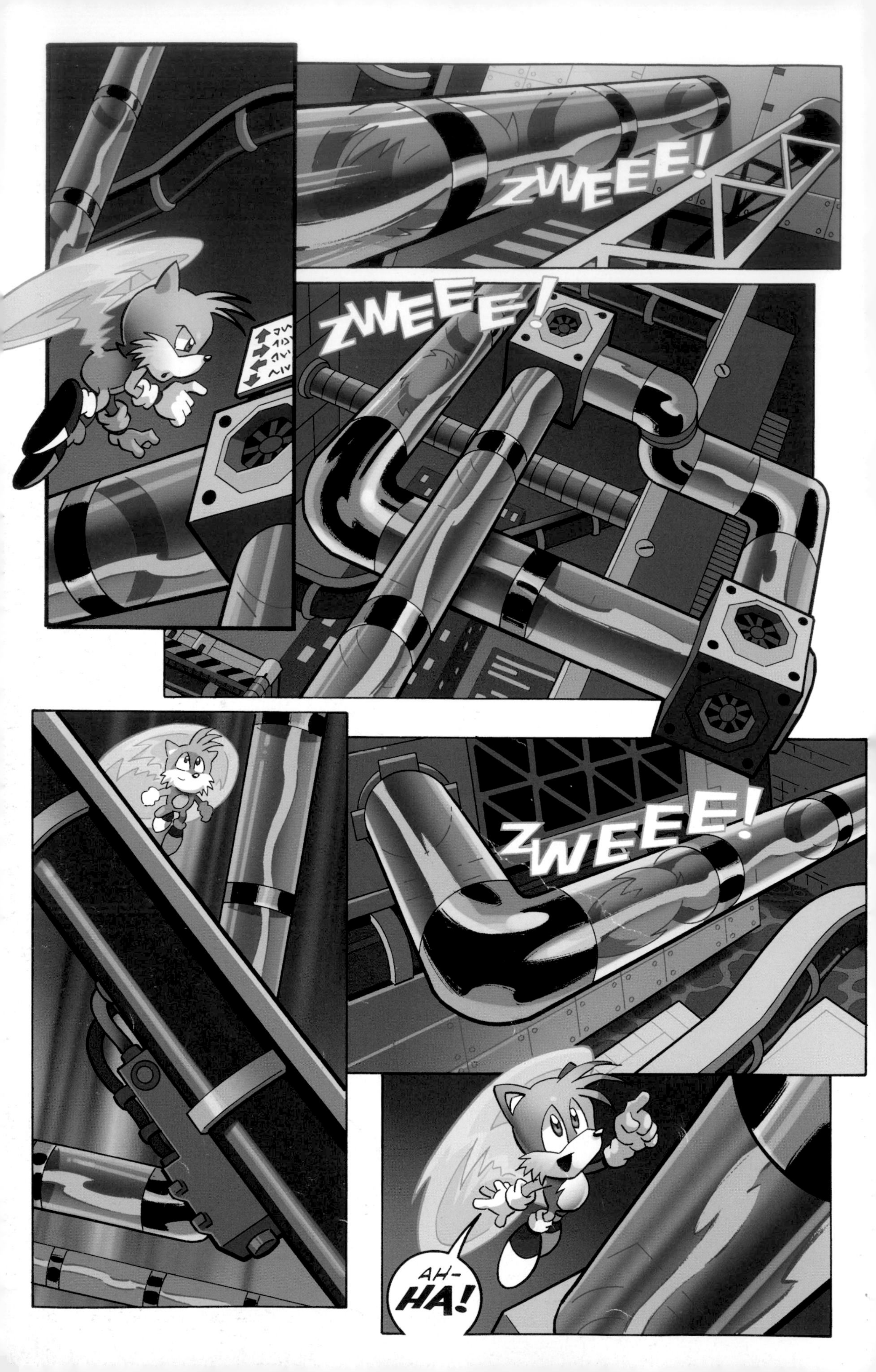
ZWEEEE!
ZWEEEE!
ZWEEEE!
AH-HA!

CHEATER! YOU FOLLOWED ME UP HERE!
HA HA! NO, I DIDN'T!
WE NEED TO GO THIS WAY!
Y'KNOW...
...YOU COULD'VE WAITED ANOTHER MINUTE, GONE AROUND THE BEND WITH US AND FOUND THIS ELEVATOR.
YEAH ...BUT WHERE WOULD THE FUN BE IN THAT?

SOON...
THIS LOOKS LIKE A SUPPLY DELIVERY ROUTE...
COOL, WE'LL JUST HOP ONE OF THESE CRATES AND RIDE OUR WAY TO THE TOP!
THEY LOOK PRETTY HEAVY. WHAT-EVER IS PULLING THEM UP SHOULD BE ENOUGH TO CARRY OUR WEIGHT, TOO!
I DON'T KNOW. THIS ALL SEEMS TOO CONVENIENT.
YOU GUYS WORRY TOO MUCH. WOO-HA!
MUST WE BE ZE LEAPING WIZOUT ZE LOOKING? LAST TIME MOI WAS NEARLY DROWN-ED.
YOU MADE IT OUT OKAY. YOU EVEN SAVED SONIC!
WAIT FOR ME! WHEEEE!
THE REAL PROBLEM IN THE LABYRINTH ZONE WAS THE--
EARTHQUAKE!

CLANG!
SHOOMP!
GLOOP!
THIS PLACE IS FILLING WITH MEGA MUCK!
I KNEW IT WOULD BE A TRAP!
MEGA-WHAT?
MEGA MUCK! A VISCOUS POLYMER WITH TOXIC PROPER-TIES!
...MEANING?
WE'RE GOING TO DROWN IN POISON SOUP!
AH.

START FLYING THEM UP. I'LL MAKE US A WAY OUT.
O-OKAY!

ANTOINE, GO! WE'LL START CLIMBING!
SALLY! COME ON!

WHAM

DOOR'S OPEN AT THE TOP!
RRRGH-- THANKS!

GO ON AHEAD! I'LL SWIM TO THE TOP!
I'M NOT LEAVING YOU BEHIND!
SOME-BODY CALL FOR A--

WHOA!
--RESCUE?

I WAS COMING BACK FOR YOU, Y'KNOW?
I THOUGHT I'D SAVE YOU THE TRIP...!

I COULD CLIMB OUT ON MY OWN...
WHERE WOULD THE FUN BE IN THAT?
WHERE INDEED?

ARE YOU OKAY? ALL "HEROED" OUT?
PANT I'M FINE. WHEW I JUST CAN'T FLY TOO LONG...

THAT TEARS IT. WE SHUT THIS PLACE DOWN, THEN FIND EGGMAN AND TEACH HIM TO TRY AND TRAP US!
LET'S NOT GET AHEAD OF OURSELVES...
DID THE FUMES GO TO YOUR HEAD?
I WANT TO END THIS QUICKLY, TOO, BUT IT'S LIKE I SAID EARLIER. WE HAVE TO CUT HIS SUPPORT LINES, OR WE'RE GOING TO BE DEALING WITH HIM OVER AND OVER AGAIN.
IF WE RUSH IN, SOMEBODY'S GOING TO GET HURT.
NOBODY'S GOING TO GET HURT AS LONG AS I'M--
SONIC...?
FINE, HAVE IT YOUR WAY. YOU GO TO THE BASES. *I'M* HEADING FOR THE BIG MAN.

SO THAT'S IT? YOU'RE JUST WALKING OUT ON US?!
I DON'T WALK. I RUN. IT'S BEEN FUN, GUYS. LATER.
UM ...I'M GOING WITH SONIC. IT WAS NICE MEETING YOU, THOUGH!
LIKE-WISE.
ANTOINE AND I WILL STICK WITH YOU, SALLY. YOU HAVEN'T LED US ASTRAY.
I AM CONFUS-ED. WERE WE JUST DUMPED?
LET'S SHUT THIS PLACE DOWN, GUYS.
SMOOTH, 'TWAN.
WHAT? THAT IS WHAT YOU ARE CALLING IT WHEN SOMEONE WALKS OUT ON YOU, *NON*?

LATER-- OIL OCEAN ZONE.
NOT TOO MUCH FURTHER, BOYS. WE SHUT THIS PLACE DOWN, AND DR. EGGMAN LOSES OVER HALF OF HIS ENERGY RESOURCES.
SAL, I'M SORRY IF THIS IS A SORE TOPIC, BUT SHOULDN'T WE HAVE MADE AN EFFORT TO KEEP SONIC AROUND?
NOT TO BELITTLE OUR EFFORTS, BUT WE COULD REALLY USE HIS SKILLS ABOUT NOW.
NO, BOOMER. YOU'RE RIGHT. I WASN'T ...I WASN'T THINKING BACK THERE...

RRRRRRRRRRRUMBLE!!!
FIRST ZE SMELL OF ZIS PLACE -URP- AND THEN ZE TREMORS...
MOBIUS IS SHAKING ITSELF APART.
THEN WE NEED TO SHUT DOWN EGGMAN'S PLANS AS FAST AS POSSIBLE.

MEANWHILE-- METROPOLIS ZONE...
WE'RE COMING UP ON DR. EGGMAN'S CITY, SONIC! IT WOULD BE NICE IF WE HAD SOME BACK-UP, DON'T YOU THINK?
NAH. IT'S BETTER THIS WAY.
THEY CAN HANDLE THEM-SELVES.
I MEANT MORE ABOUT US. WE'RE IN WAY OVER OUR HEADS...
DON'T SWEAT IT, LITTLE BRO'! YOU JUST KEEP THE TORNADO SAFE WHILE I RUIN EGGMAN'S DAY! THEN WE'LL FLY OFF TO OUR HAPPILY-EVER-AFTER.
IF YOU SAY SO...
I'LL HAVE MY RADIO ON SO WE CAN KEEP IN TOUCH. SEE YOU IN A BIT!

NOW-- TO HANDLE THE DOC WHILE EVERY-ONE ELSE IS AT A SAFE DISTANCE.
READY OR NOT, EGGMAN! HERE I COME!
YOU CAN'T STOP NOW, SONIC--YOU'RE IN EGGMAN COUNTRY!
IT'S THE SHOWDOWN YOU'VE BEEN WAITING FOR, AND THE STAKES ARE HIGH!
THE FATE OF THE WORLD--OF REALITY ITSELF --HANGS IN THE BALANCE!
UNTIL NEXT TIME, HEAD OVER TO ARCHIECOMICS.COM TO GET THE FULL SCOOP ON OUR SISTER TITLE SONIC UNIVERSE,
AND ALL THE BRAND NEW GRAPHIC NOVELS HEADING YOUR WAY--INCLUDING KNUCKLES ARCHIVES, SONIC LEGACY, SONIC UNIVERSE: VOLUME 1, SONIC ARCHIVES, AND SONIC SELECTS!!!

SONIC GENESIS

PART FOUR

SPAZ AFTER LEE

TAKE A GLIMPSE AT A *WHOLE NEW WORLD*...ONE *DIFFERENT* FROM WHAT YOU KNOW FROM THE *SEGA GAMES* AND THE *COMICS!* -- WHERE WE ENTER THE EVER-CHANGING ADVENTURES OF A *SPEEDY BLUE HERO* NAMED ***SONIC THE HEDGEHOG!***

Genesis
Part Four: RESET

WRITER: IAN FLYNN
PENCILS: TRACY YARDLEY!
INKS: TERRY AUSTIN
COLORS: MATT HERMS
LETTERS: JOHN WORKMAN
COVER BY PATRICK SPAZIANTE
EDITOR: PAUL KAMINSKI
EDITOR-IN-CHIEF: VICTOR GORELICK
PRESIDENT: MIKE PELLERITO
SPECIAL THANKS TO *CINDY CHAU* AND *JUDY GILBERTSON* AT *SEGA LICENSING*

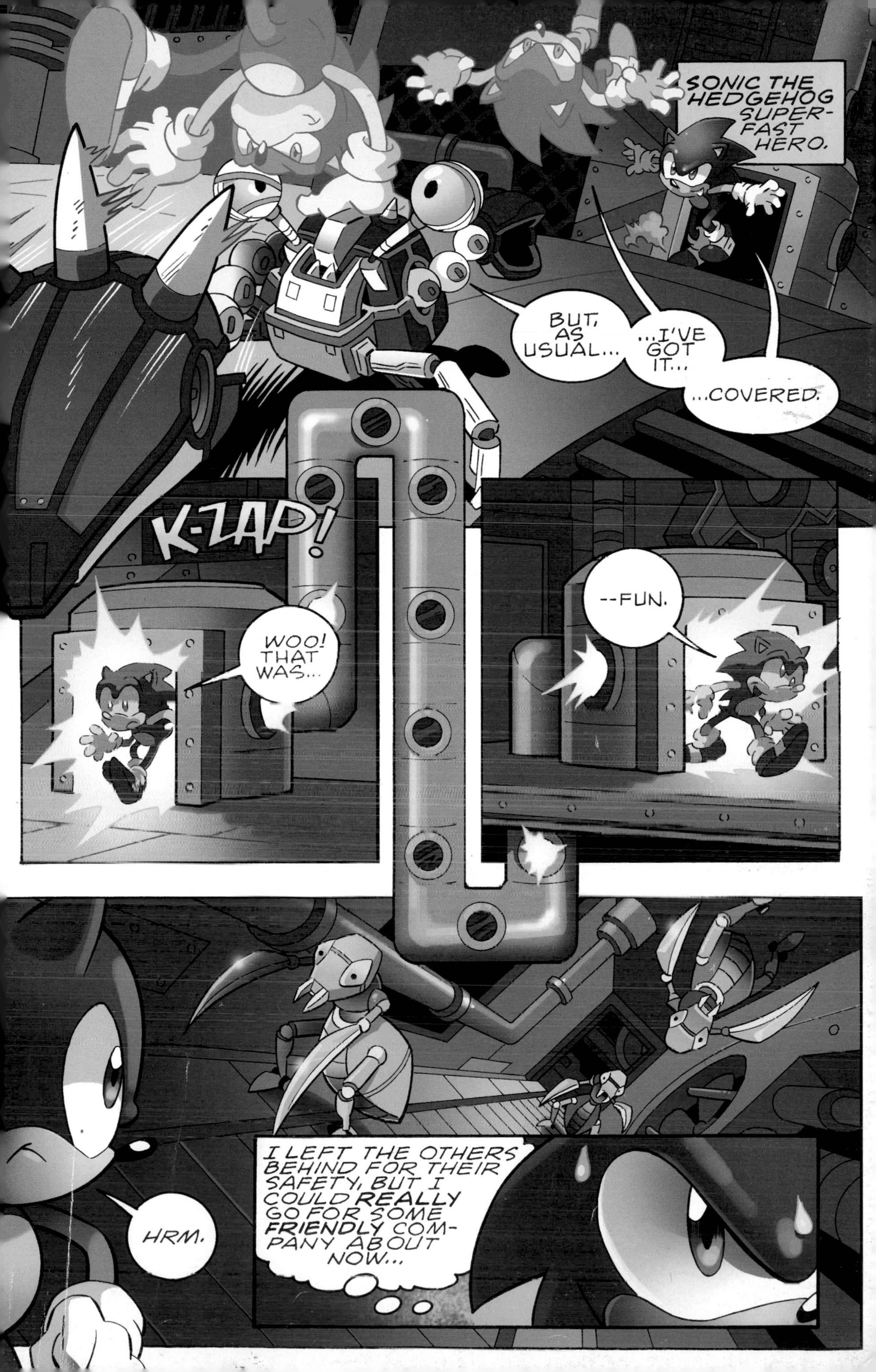
SONIC THE HEDGEHOG SUPER-FAST HERO.
BUT, AS USUAL...
...I'VE GOT IT...
...COVERED.
K-ZAP!
WOO! THAT WAS...
--FUN.
HRM.
I LEFT THE OTHERS BEHIND FOR THEIR SAFETY, BUT I COULD REALLY GO FOR SOME FRIENDLY COMPANY ABOUT NOW...

OIL OCEAN ZONE.
THIS WAY! RUN FOR COVER!
BETWEEN THOSE CONTAINERS! HURRY!
MAN, I WISH WE'D CONVINCED SONIC TO STICK WITH US!
YOU'RE RIGHT! I SHOULD'VE TRIED HARDER TO REASON WITH HIM. SOMETHING TELLS ME HE SHOULD BE HERE WITH ME!
US! BE HERE WITH US!
UH-HUH!

MAYBE I WILL BE FACING ZE ROBOTS. MAYBE THEN I WILL BE GETTING ZE ATTENTION I--

ZAP
GYEEP!
ZAP
ZAP

CLANG!

WHAT ARE THOSE?! WHAT ARE THEY EVEN *FOR*?!
INCOMING! NINE O'CLOCK HIGH!

AIEEE EEEE!
GRAB MY HAND!
HOLD ON!
I--
THOOMP
--I RE-MEMBER!
YIPE!
KA-BLAM
IT'S ALL COMING BACK...LIKE A DREAM...
NYAGH!
RIP SONIC
KA-BLAM

OW!
KABLAM!
SPLAT!
THAT WAS AWE-SOME!
NON. AWESOME IS NOT MOVING. MAKE ZE WORLD STOP MOVING, S'IL VOUS PLAIT.
AND NOW IT'S GONE. FOCUS, SALLY, FOCUS.
EXCUSE ME, LITTLE ONE. MY FRIENDS AND I ARE TRYING TO SHUT THIS PLACE DOWN AND RESCUE EVERYONE. DO YOU HAPPEN TO KNOW WHERE THE MAIN VALVES ARE?
ALL RIGHT! NOW WE'RE GETTING SOME-WHERE! LET'S FINISH THIS!

"AND BACK UP SONIC!"
NEAR-DEATH EXPERIENCES AND CLOSE SHAVES WITH BADNIKS ASIDE, THIS PLACE AIN'T HALF BAD.
NOT THAT "LIFE-CONSUMING INDUSTRIAL WASTELAND" IS MY THING, BUT...
AND HERE I THOUGHT EGGMAN WAS THE BIGGEST NUT IN THIS PLACE.
HA HA HA! AH...ONE MORE REASON I NEED THE OTHERS HERE. THERE'S NOBODY TO LAUGH AT MY JOKES.
MIGHT HAVE TO TRANSLATE IT FOR 'TWAN INTO "*DWEEB-ESE*!" BOOMER WOULD'VE LIKED IT. SALLY...

...WOULD SCOLD ME FOR RUNNING INTO A TRAP. HOO BOY.
NOW, THE QUESTION IS: WHICH IS FASTER? YOUR DETONATORS...
POW
...OR ME?
YEAH, I KNOW, STUPID QUESTION.

BRAVO! YOU'VE GONE TO A LOT OF EFFORT TO GET TO ME, RODENT!
AT LEAST YOU'RE MAN ENOUGH TO MEET ME FACE TO...
..."RODENT"...?
YOU'VE CALLED ME THAT BEFORE.
...WE'VE BEEN DOING THIS FOR A LOT LONGER THAN A FEW DAYS...
SO YOU'VE FINALLY BEGUN TO REMEMBER, HAVE YOU? WELL, WE CAN'T HAVE THAT.
REPLICAS --DEPLOY!
COME AND GET ME, SONIC!

MEANWHILE, IN THE OIL OCEAN ZONE...
...OKAY, THAT CUTS THE FEED TO THIS REGION...
-WHEW- I HAVE SHUTTED OFF ZIS PIPELINE.
AND I GOT THE REST. NO MORE OIL IS FLOWING.
YOU GUYS ARE THE BEST! WITH THE FLOW STOPPED AND THE LINES SHUT DOWN...
"...EGGMAN LOSES POWER TO ALL HIS BASES IN THIS ENTIRE REGION!"

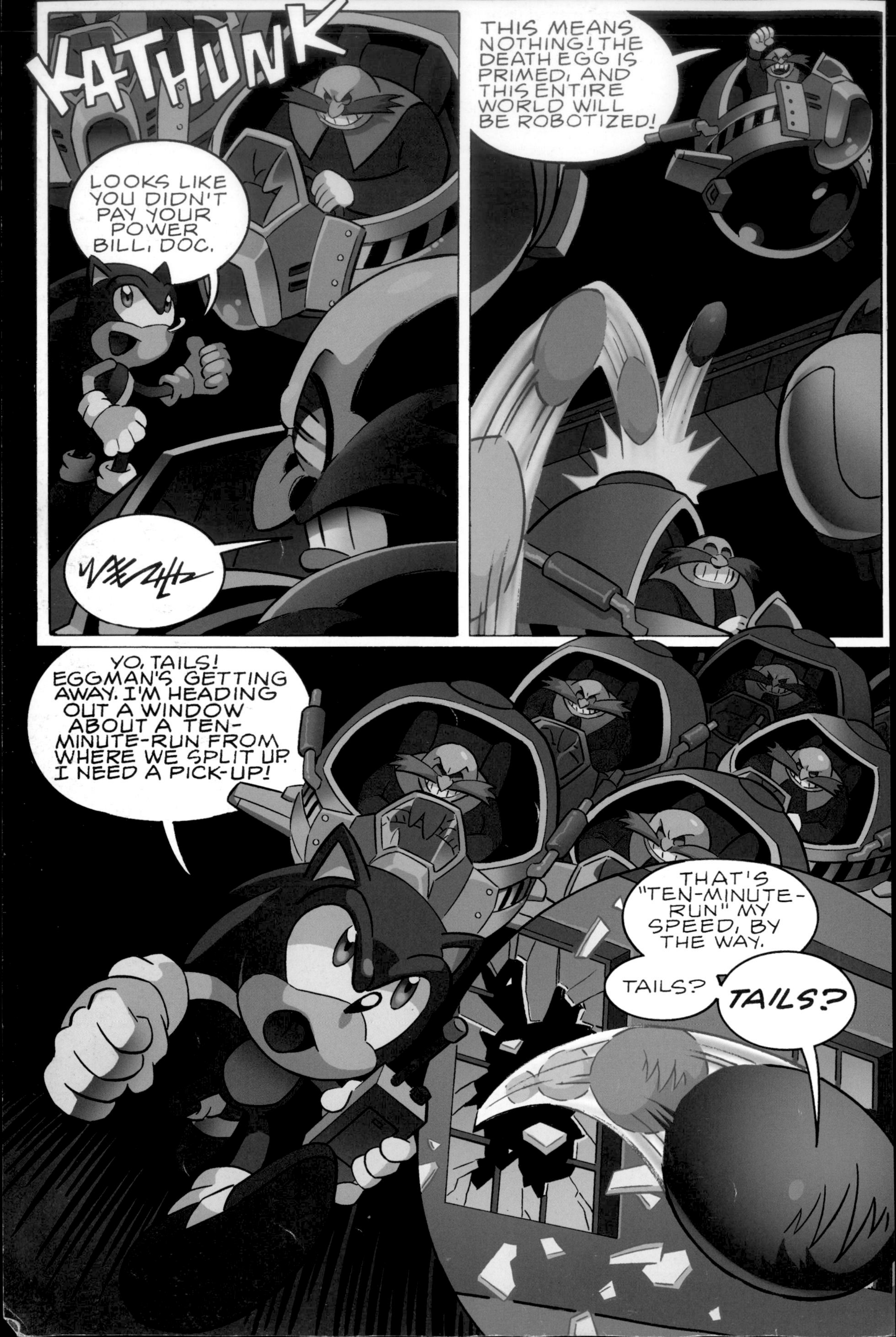
KATHUNK
LOOKS LIKE YOU DIDN'T PAY YOUR POWER BILL, DOC.
THIS MEANS NOTHING! THE DEATH EGG IS PRIMED, AND THIS ENTIRE WORLD WILL BE ROBOTIZED!
YO, TAILS! EGGMAN'S GETTING AWAY. I'M HEADING OUT A WINDOW ABOUT A TEN-MINUTE-RUN FROM WHERE WE SPLIT UP. I NEED A PICK-UP!
THAT'S "TEN-MINUTE-RUN" MY SPEED, BY THE WAY.
TAILS?
TAILS?

NICE DRAMATIC TIMING, KID.
HAHAHA! SORRY!
YOU NEED TO GIVE ME MORE WARNING NEXT TIME!
YOW! TALK ABOUT TIM-ING!
A COUPLE OF DAYS AGO, THE TREMORS WERE JUST ANNOYING SHAKE-UPS.
THIS IS GETTING OUT OF HAND.
RRRRUMBLE!
DOES THIS MEAN DR. EGGMAN *WASN'T* THE CAUSE OF THE EARTHQUAKES? OR ARE WE JUST TOO LATE?
NO, THIS IS ALL HIS FAULT. AND IT'S *NEVER* TOO LATE. WE JUST HAVE TO FIND HIM... AND...
...*OH*, WELL, THAT WAS EASY.

I'LL GET YOU AS CLOSE TO THE DECK AS I CAN!
DON'T BOTHER.
THE WHOLE THING IS A DECOY...
"...HE'S MAKING A BREAK FOR THE DEATH EGG!"
"THE WHAT?"
SONIC!

COUGH! HACK! NOT ONE OF MY BRIGHTER MOMENTS...
...WHOA. IT'S NOT JUST EARTH-QUAKES. THE WHOLE PLANET IS TEARING APART...
INDEED.
IT'S TRYING DESPERATELY TO RETURN TO WHAT IT ONCE WAS. BUT WHEN I FIRE THE DEATH EGG'S ROBOTIZER...
...IT WILL CEMENT THE DIMENSIONAL SHIFT, AS WELL AS TURN EVERY LIVING THING...
...INTO MY ROBOT SLAVE.

SO THERE WAS ANOTHER WORLD! AND THERE'S STILL A CHANCE TO SET THINGS RIGHT!
THERE WAS, BUT I'VE CHANGED IT TO BE PRIMED FOR MY CONQUEST...!
AND WHILE YOU MIGHT HAVE HAD A CHANCE BEFORE...
...IT'S TOO LATE NOW!

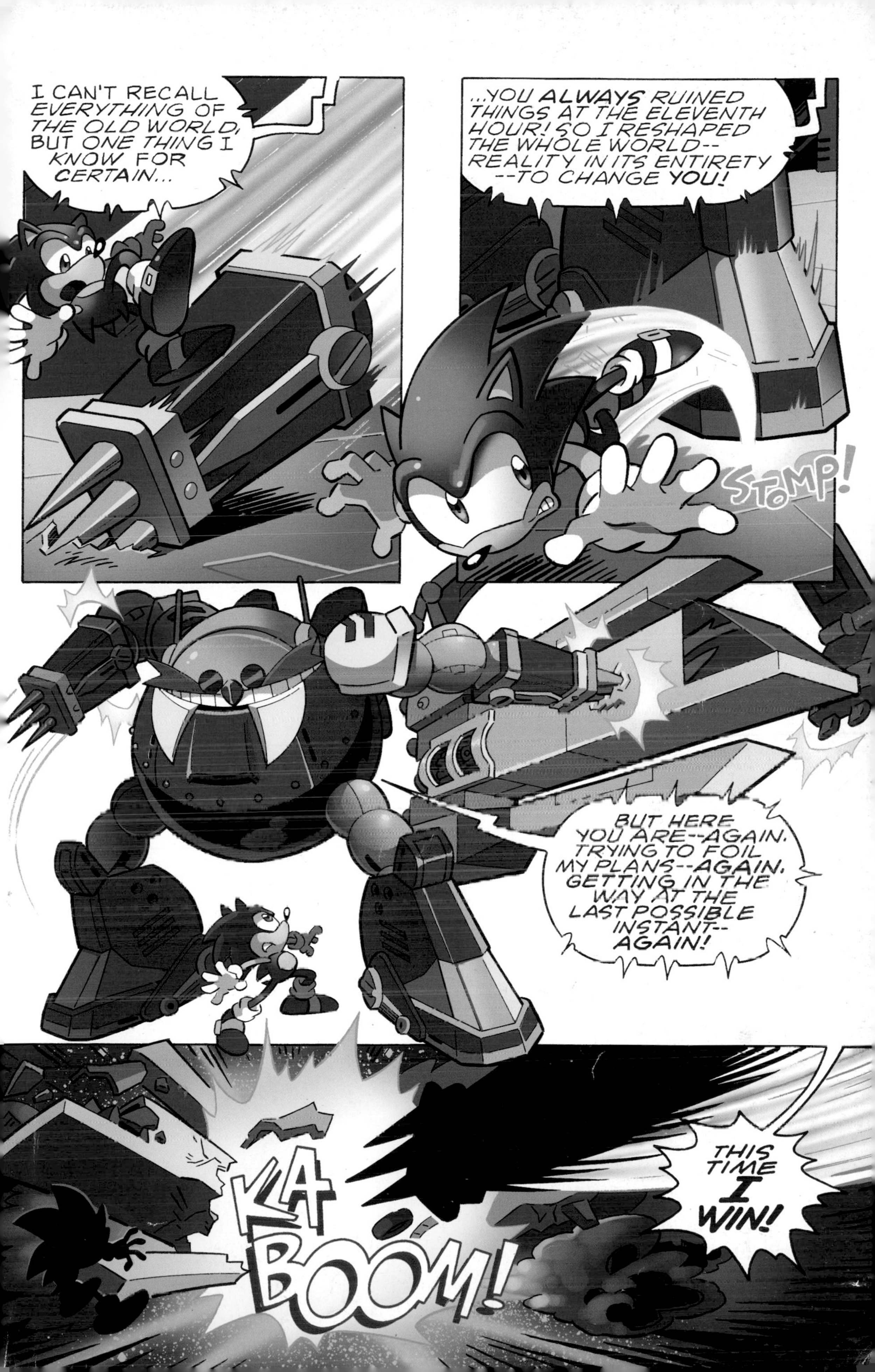
I CAN'T RECALL EVERYTHING OF THE OLD WORLD, BUT ONE THING I KNOW FOR CERTAIN...
...YOU ALWAYS RUINED THINGS AT THE ELEVENTH HOUR! SO I RESHAPED THE WHOLE WORLD-- REALITY IN ITS ENTIRETY --TO CHANGE YOU!
STOMP!
BUT HERE YOU ARE--AGAIN. TRYING TO FOIL MY PLANS--AGAIN. GETTING IN THE WAY AT THE LAST POSSIBLE INSTANT-- AGAIN!
KA BOOM!
THIS TIME I WIN!

YOU'RE BEAT, RODENT. I HOLD ALL THE ACES. I HAVE MY DEATH EGG. IT'S POWERED BY ALL THE CHAOS EMERALDS. YOU **CANNOT** BEAT ME!
...POWERED BY THE CHAOS EMERALDS... ?
GOOD-BYE, SONIC!
Y'KNOW, DOC...
FWASH!
...SOMETIMES YOU MAKE THIS **TOO** EASY.

NO! NO!
IT'S NOT POSSIBLE! A DIRECT CURRENT LIKE THAT SHOULD'VE FRIED YOU!
DUDE, YOU'RE THE ONE WHO TOLD ME WHAT KIND OF JUICE WAS RUNNING THROUGH THOSE CABLES.
RRRARGH!
WHOA. BRILLIANT COME BACK. YOU'RE A GENIUS, ALL RIGHT.
HATE YOU! HATE YOU! ALL OF MY HATE! DIE! DIE! DIE!

DOCTOR EGGMAN? UNCLE? SIR? W-WE HAVE A PROBLEM...
THE DIMENSIONAL STABILITY IS DEGRADING EXPONENTIALLY. I DON'T THINK EVEN THE ROBOTIZER'S EFFECTS WILL STOP IT. AND WHATEVER'S GOING ON AT YOUR POSITION IS MAKING IT WORSE...
EEK!
DO YOU HEAR ME?! THE WORLD IS TEARING ITSELF APART, AND WE CAN'T STOP IT...!
THEN I BETTER HURRY UP WHILE THERE'S STILL A PLANET TO SAVE.

FIRST, I NEED YOU OUT OF THE WAY.
WHAM
ARGH! CURSE YOU!
SECOND, I'M GOING TO NEED TO TAP INTO AS MUCH CHAOS POWER AS I CAN. THIS IS USUALLY THAT OTHER GUY'S SHTICK...SHADY? STREAKY? WHAT-EVER.
MAYBE...I CAN SET THINGS RIGHT. MAYBE EVEN GO BACK FAR ENOUGH TO SAVE HER. IF CHAOS GOT US HERE, CHAOS CAN GET US BACK, AND I CAN'T BOTHER WITH SECOND GUESSES. I'M OUT OF TIME AND OUT OF OPTIONS, SO...HERE GOES.
CHAOS CONTROL!

THERE... IT'S DONE. WE'LL SEE WHAT HAPPENS NOW.
Hi SAL
SALLY! EVERYTHING'S VANISHING! WHAT DO WE DO?!
IT'S OKAY, ROTOR. SONIC HAS EVERYTHING UNDER CONTROL.
SONIC? "ROTOR" ?!
TRUST ME. EVERYTHING WILL BE OKAY.
SEE YOU, SONIC...
...ON THE OTHER SIDE, SALLY.

SONIC: GENESIS
EPILOGUE

WELCOME TO THE PLANET MOBIUS--A WORLD UNIQUE AND BEYOND WHAT YOU KNOW FROM THE SEGA GAMES!-- WHERE SONIC AND THE HEROIC FREEDOM FIGHTERS WORK TO SAVE THE WORLD FROM THE FORCES OF EVIL!
ALL OF THIS WAS SEEN IN "SONIC-GENESIS" IN STH #226-229.
THERE WAS A FLASH OF LIGHT... AND THEN I WAS SOME-WHERE...
...NEW...
...BUT FAMILIAR!
I MET ALL THESE NEW FRIENDS...
...BUT I ALREADY KNEW THEM!
THERE WAS A HUGE FIGHT, AND THEN I...
...I NEEDED MORE TIME TO...
HI SAL

SALLY!
RIGHT! TEN-SECOND REWIND!
NO CHEAP SHOT FOR YOU!
TWO STEPS BACK...
SONIC! WE'RE OUT OF TIME! WE'VE GOT TOOO-OOP!
?!
WAY AHEAD OF YOU, SAL!
Writer: IAN FLYNN • Pencils: BEN BATES
Inks: TERRY AUSTIN • Colors: MATT HERMS
Letters: JOHN WORKMAN
Cover: BEN BATES
Variant Cover Art Provided by SEGA
Editor: PAUL KAMINSKI
Editor-in-Chief: VICTOR GORELICK
President: MIKE PELLERITO
Special thanks to CINDY CHAU, and JUDY GILBERTSON at SEGA Licensing

SONIC! THERE'S A--!
LIKE I JUST SAID...
BLAM
BLAM
BLAM
...WAY AHEAD OF YOU, SAL.
WHAT'S THE MATTER? TOO MUCH AWESOME CONDENSED INTO ONE MOMENT?
...NO, IT'S ...IT'S NOT THAT...
F22
HI SAL
...IT'S NOTHING. LET'S KEEP MOVING.

MEANWHILE
WHY ISN'T IT WORKING ?
SNIVELY! WHY ISN'T THE COSMIC RESET BUTTON RESETTING THE COSMOS?
I-I-I DON'T KNOW, SIR! I'M NOT READING ANY PROBLEMS! IT'S JUST...
...NOT WORKING?
RRRRARGH! HOW AM I SUPPOSED TO ROBOTIZE A COMPLETELY HELPLESS AND REBOOTED WORLD IF IT'S NOT HELPLESSLY REBOOTED?!
D-DON'T YOU MEAN "ROBOTICIZED," SIR?
SHUT IT!

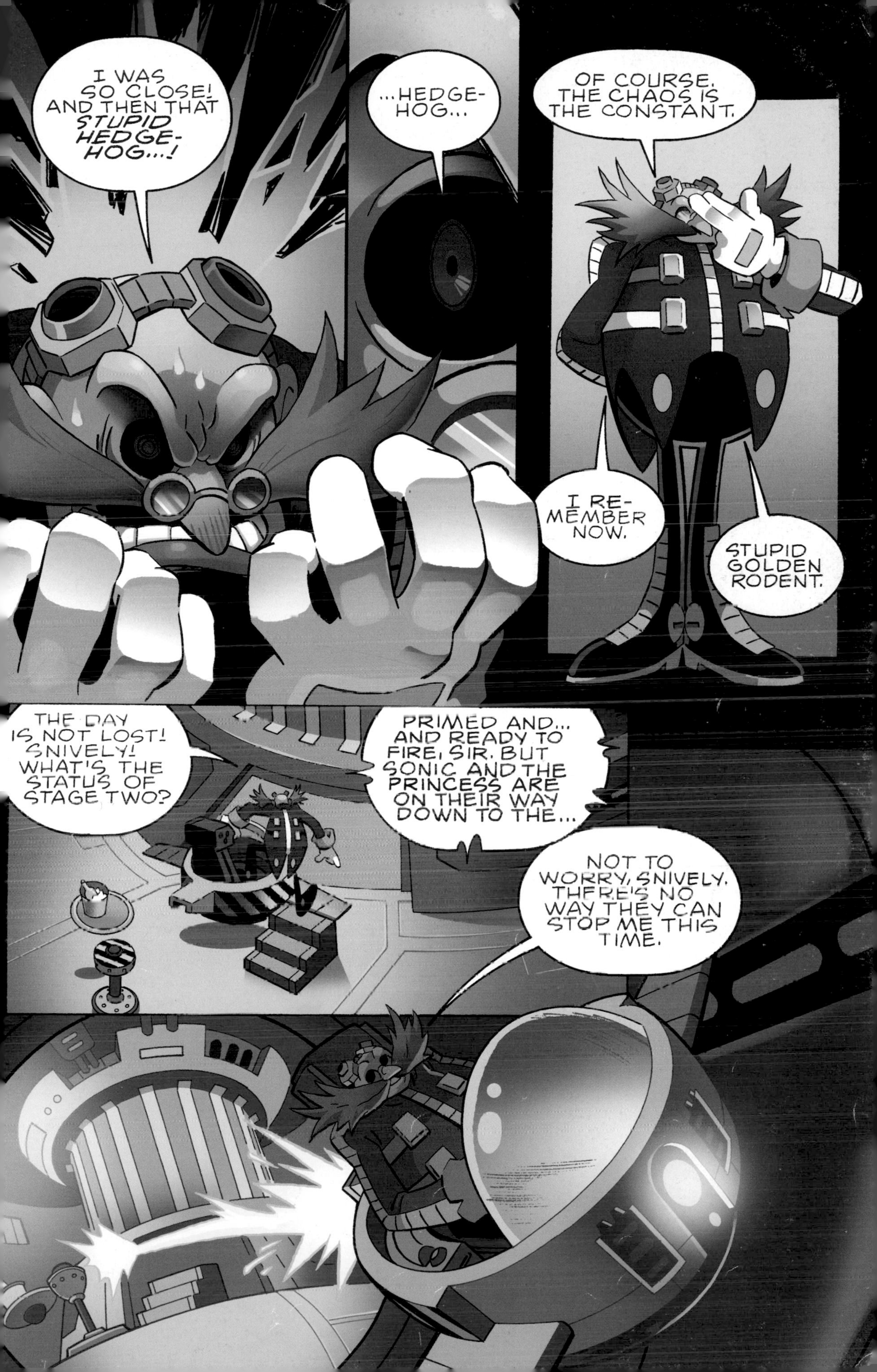
I WAS SO CLOSE! AND THEN THAT STUPID HEDGE-HOG...!
...HEDGE-HOG...
OF COURSE. THE CHAOS IS THE CONSTANT.
I RE-MEMBER NOW.
STUPID GOLDEN RODENT.
THE DAY IS NOT LOST! SNIVELY! WHAT'S THE STATUS OF STAGE TWO?
PRIMED AND... AND READY TO FIRE, SIR. BUT SONIC AND THE PRINCESS ARE ON THEIR WAY DOWN TO THE...
NOT TO WORRY, SNIVELY. THERE'S NO WAY THEY CAN STOP ME THIS TIME.

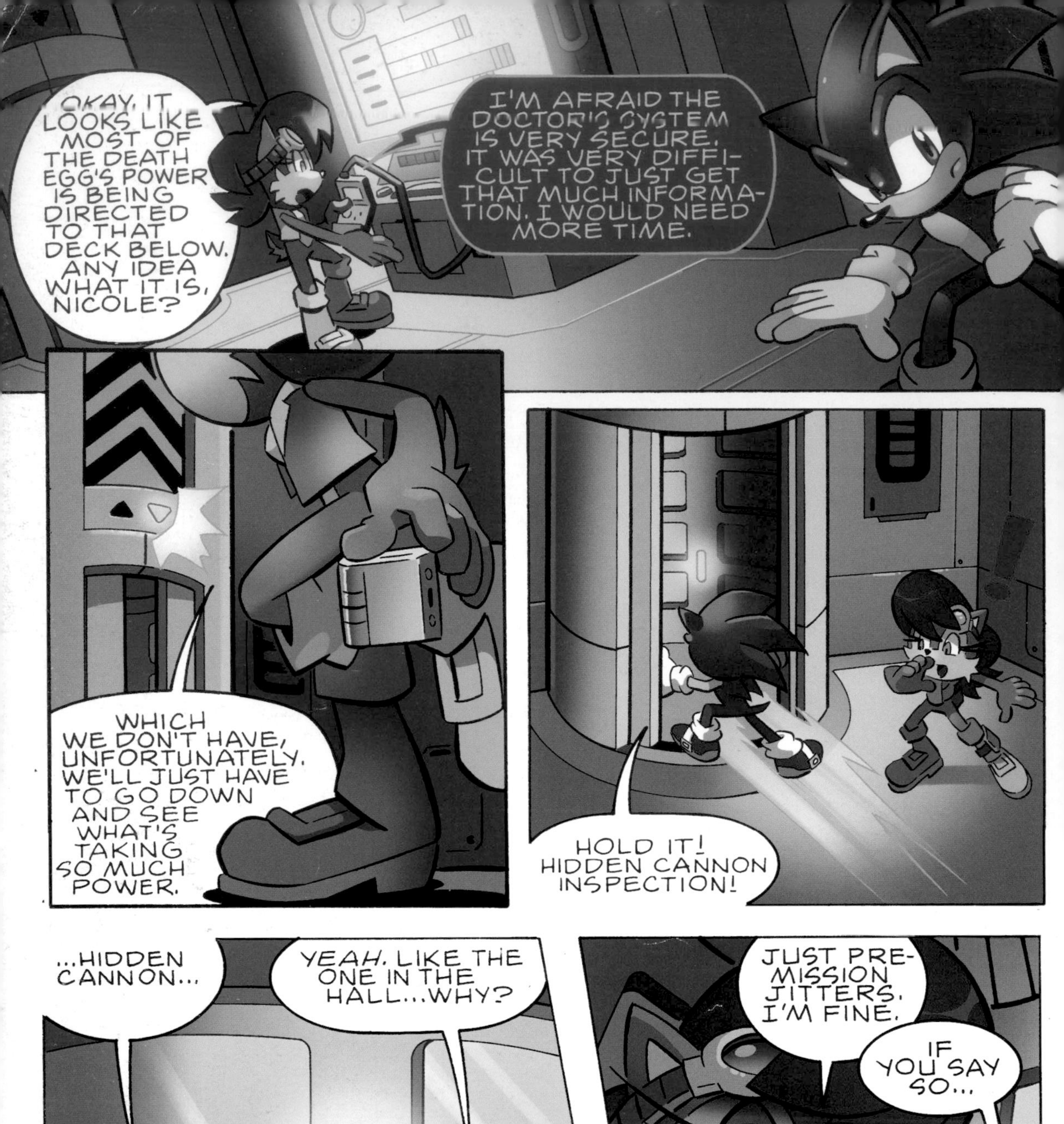
OKAY, IT LOOKS LIKE MOST OF THE DEATH EGG'S POWER IS BEING DIRECTED TO THAT DECK BELOW. ANY IDEA WHAT IT IS, NICOLE?
I'M AFRAID THE DOCTOR'S SYSTEM IS VERY SECURE. IT WAS VERY DIFFI-CULT TO JUST GET THAT MUCH INFORMA-TION. I WOULD NEED MORE TIME.
WHICH WE DON'T HAVE, UNFORTUNATELY. WE'LL JUST HAVE TO GO DOWN AND SEE WHAT'S TAKING SO MUCH POWER.
HOLD IT! HIDDEN CANNON INSPECTION!

...HIDDEN CANNON...
YEAH. LIKE THE ONE IN THE HALL...WHY?
JUST PRE-MISSION JITTERS. I'M FINE.
IF YOU SAY SO...

YOWZA!
THAT LOOKS LIKE A GIANT ROBOTICIZER!
PSHHHHT! HA HA HA HA!
A WORLD ROBOTICIZER, TO BE PRECISE.
AND HERE I THOUGHT WE HAD SOMETHING TO WORRY ABOUT! YOU REMEMBER THOSE ALIENS THAT SNAGGED US A WHILE BACK?* WHEN THEY DEROBOTICIZED EVERYONE, THEY MADE SURE IT WAS FOR KEEPS!
*StH # 118.

YES, YES.
THOSE BOTHERSOME BEM. THEY RE-WROTE THE RULES OF THE GAME. BUT I CHANGED THEM BACK.
YOU'RE BLUFFING.
SURELY YOU NOTICED THE FLASH OF LIGHT? THE MOMENTARY DISORIENTATION? THAT WAS JUST PHASE ONE!
EVERY-THING DID RESET... RIGHT...?
SIMULATION
I HEARD THAT. REGARDLESS, DO YOU RECALL, DEAR PRINCESS, WHAT HAPPENS WHEN YOU TRY TO ROBOTICIZE SOMETHING THAT'S ALREADY MECHANICAL?
WHAT'S HE TALKING ABOUT?
WHEN I TRICKED HIM INTO ROBOTICIZING MY AUTO AUTOMATON DOUBLE.*
OH, NO...
*PRINCESS SALLY MINI-SERIES.
THAT'S RIGHT! IT EXPLODES! ALL OF G.U.N.'S FORCES! ALL OF THE UNITED FED-ERATION BLOWN BACK TO THE STONE AGE.
HA HAHAHA HA!
SIMULATION

AND LET'S NOT FORGET NEW MOBOTROPOLIS! THERE GOES YOUR PRECIOUS NANITE-MADE CITY! HAHA HA HA HA!
...DAD...
BUNNIE ...AND NICOLE ...!
OKAY, I TAKE BACK THE LAUGHING...
WAIT!
YOU'LL DESTROY EVERY CHAPTER OF YOUR DARK EGG LEGION!
WHAT'S YOUR POINT? I'LL HAVE MILLIONS OF ROBOT SLAVES TO REBUILD MY ROBOT ARMY. BESIDES...
...YOU CAN'T MAKE AN OMELET WITHOUT BREAKING A FEW DARK EGG LEGION-NAIRES.

I NEVER SHOULD'VE SHOWN YOU A SHRED OF MERCY, YOU SICK--!
AH-AH-AH! LANGUAGE, RODENT!
HRK! OKAY! I'M OFFICIALLY GETTING TIRED OF METAL SONICS!
I REALLY DON'T HAVE TIME TO MESS WITH--
--YOU.
THOOM

HAHAHA! HAVING TROUBLE, RODENT?

NO WORDS OF ENCOURAGEMENT, PRIN--? BLAST IT! WHERE DID SHE GO?!

I'LL TOLERATE THE HEDGEHOG CAUSING PROBLEMS. THAT'S JUST A FACT OF LIFE. BUT YOU AREN'T ALLOWED TO INTERFERE WITH--
EGAD!
I KNOW YOU'VE GOT A PLAN, SAL!
I'LL TRY TO KEEP THESE GUYS BUSY...

"...WHILE YOU SAVE THE DAY!"
DID THAT DO IT? ARE YOU PATCHED INTO THE NETWORK?
I AM. BUT THE DEFENSIVE SOFT-WARE REMAINS FORMIDABLE. IT WILL TAKE HOURS TO BREAK THE ENCRYPTION.
WE HAVE *MINUTES.*
CAN WE BLOCK THE COMMAND SIGNAL? CON-FUSE START-UP PROCESSES?
NO.
I AM LOCKED OUT, AND IT IS READY TO FIRE. I COULD POTENTIALLY *INVERT* THE BEAM, **TO THIS EXACT POINT,** BUT...

DO IT.
BUT YOU WILL NOT BE IMMUNE...
MAKE SURE YOUR CORE PROGRAMS...
...ARE SAFE AT HOME.
JUST GIVE ME A MANUAL EXECUTABLE.
BUT YOU WILL BE...

NICOLE... I'VE BEEN GIVEN A SECOND CHANCE. I CAN SAVE EVERYONE WITH THAT.
PLEASE ...I CAN'T DO THIS WITHOUT YOU.

SAL...! IF YOU'RE GONNA DO SOMETHING, DO IT NOW!
NO MORE SET-BACKS! SNIVELY! FIRE THE WORLD ROBOTI-CIZER!
•A.I. DOWNLOAD TO NEW MOBOTROPOLIS SERVER: COMPLETE
•BEAM INVERSE OVERRIDE: COMPLETE
•GOOD BYE, MY FRIEND
•EXECUTE? Y N
GOOD-BYE...

VVVVMMMMMMMMMMMMM
YES!
VVVVMMMMMMMMMMM
NO! NO!!!
KA THOOM
SWEET!
SONIC AND SALLY MUST'VE DONE SOME- THING!

=KZZT= YOU READ ME, SIR?! =KZZT=

THERE =KZZT!= MASSIVE ENERGY LEAKS IN ALL SYSTEMS! THE ROBOTICIZER ISN'T JUST OFF-LINE--IT'S GONE! =KZZT!=

=KZZT!= ALL OTHER SYSTEMS ARE STILL ON-LINE. NO LOSS IN ALTITUDE =KZZT= AND THE POWER RING MATRIX IS HOLDING. BARELY.

I GUESS THE OLD IMMUNITY WASN'T RESET AFTER ALL. OH, PLEASE... **PLEASE** TELL ME THAT FINISHED HIM OFF...
CLANG!
NO. OF COURSE NOT.
HEY. LOOK. WE WIN. **AGAIN.**

NOT... YET!
YOU'RE STILL ...YOU'RE STILL ON MY TURF, RODENT... AND... AND...
DUDE, COME ON. WE WIN. I'M GONNA FIND SALLY. THEN WE'RE DESTROYING YOUR DUMB EGG.
THEN I'M STOMPING ON NAUGUS. AND THEN THE TWO OF YOU CAN ROT IN A CELL.
AND THEN I'M GOING TO EAT A MILLION CHILI DOGS. AND THEN...
...OH, NO. OH, NO, NO, NO, NO!
AH...AH-HA! HA-HA-HA! HAHAHA!

HAHAHAHAHAHAHAHA
HAHAHAHAHAHA
BWA
HEDGEHOG. PRIORITY ONE.
HAHAHA
TO BE CONTINUED IN CURRENT ISSUES OF
SONIC THE HEDGEHOG
&
SONIC UNIVERSE
AVAILABLE AT
ARCHIECOMICS.COM

AFTERWORD

Hey there, Sonic fans! What did you think of "Sonic: Genesis"? Pretty cool, right? It's been a long, wild ride to get to the gorgeous book you hold in your hands right now. Originally, the story was going to go from the events of Sonic the Hedgehog #225 straight into what you read in Sonic the Hedgehog #230. But editor Paul Kaminski said: "This is Sonic's 20th anniversary. The Sonic fans deserve more than that!" "More than the return of the Death Egg, Sally put in mortal peril, and King Naugus?" I asked. "Yes!" he said.

Right about that time, SEGA contacted us and let us know that Sonic Generations was on the way, and that Sonic would be returning to his 2-D roots. What better way of remembering Sonic's history by reliving his origin story?

Even when we had locked in the general idea, it went through a number of revisions. Every branch of SEGA, from the American to the European to the Japanese divisions, all helped weigh in on the project. Should it be its own story? Should it be a Sonic Generations adaptation? Should it be a stand-alone issue? Should it be nine issues long? Should it be in-continuity, out-of-continuity, or somewhere in between? You hold the end result. Not too shabby, eh?

This afterword is a shout-out to all you fans who made this such a success. Even before "Sonic: Genesis" hit the stands, the hype was incredible. Feedback for the first part was so positive it gave us the opportunity to make this book. And if you all demand it, we can return to the world of "Genesis" for more game-inspired adventures. You, the awesome fan base and readership, make this possible and shape the future!

I also want to thank the art team for taking my script and rendering such an amazing story. It was a thrill to work with the legendary Patrick "Spaz" Spaziante, whose artwork in the classic issues and comic covers first got me reading the comic. It's always a pleasure to see the pencils of the amazingly versatile Tracy Yardley! We joined the book at the same time, and he's never failed to impress me with his skills. Terry Austin took all their lines and gave them life, while John Workman took my words and put them in their proper place in the universe. And I can't fail to mention the absolutely gorgeous colors by my good buddy Matt Herms.

So thanks to all of you and all of them for making "Sonic: Genesis" such an awesome experience!

See you for more adventures across Mobius!
Ian Flynn

IAN
FLYNN

SPECIAL STAGE

WELCOME TO THE SPECIAL FEATURES SECTION! YOU HAVE JUST READ ONE OF THE MOST EPIC ADVENTURES OUR HERO HAS EVER EMBARKED ON. WE THOUGHT YOU'D LIKE TO LEARN A LITTLE MORE ABOUT HOW "GENESIS" WAS MADE.

TAKE A CLOSER LOOK AT THE EVOLUTION OF "GENESIS"!

BREAK-DOWN PENCILS BY SPAZ

FINISHED PENCILS BY TRACY YARDLEY!

INKS BY TERRY AUSTIN AND LETTERS BY JOHN WORKMAN

FINISHED COLOR ART BY MATT HERMS

SONIC THE HEDGEHOG #226 PAGE 1

SEE HOW A PAGE GOES FROM SKETCH TO FINAL COLORS!

BREAK-DOWN PENCILS BY SPAZ

FINISHED PENCILS BY TRACY YARDLEY!

INKS BY TERRY AUSTIN AND LETTERS BY JOHN WORKMAN

FINISHED COLOR ART BY MATT HERMS

SONIC THE HEDGEHOG #227 PAGE 1

STH #225 COVER BY
PATRICK "SPAZ" SPAZINATE

Tracy Yardley!
STH #225 VARIANT COVER
BY TRACY YARDLEY!

SONIC THE HEDGEHOG
#226 CONVENTION COVER

SONIC THE HEDGEHOG
#230 VARIANT COVER

GENESIS PENCIL COVERS BY PATRICK "SPAZ" SPAZIANTE

GENESIS I

GENESIS II

GENESIS III

ALTERNATE GENESIS II

CONVENTION EXCLUSIVE
GENESIS IV PENCIL COVER
BY PATRICK "SPAZ" SPAZIANTE

SONIC GENESIS
PART FOUR

SPAZ

SONIC #225 COVER PRODUCTION ART

STH #225 VARIANT COVER CONCEPT ART BY TRACY YARDLEY!

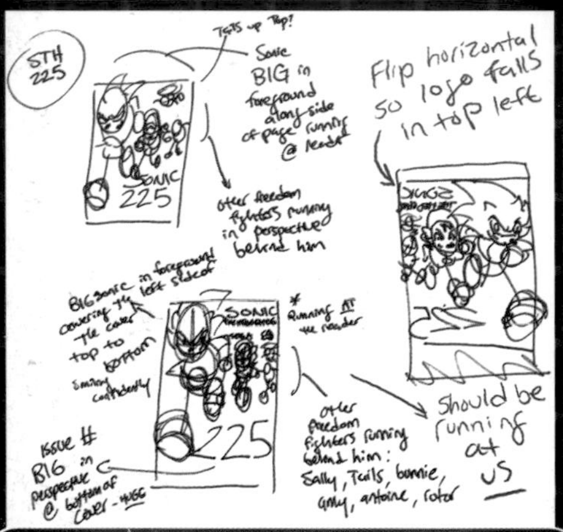

SKETCH CONCEPTS FOR STH #225 MAIN COVER BY PAUL KAMINSKI

DIFFERENT TAKES ON SONIC'S WORRIED EXPRESSION BY TRACY YARDLEY!

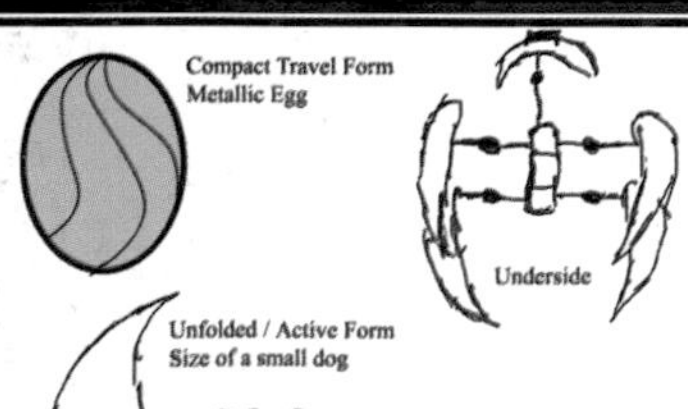

EGG MITE CONCEPT ART BY IAN FLYNN

SONIC #225 COVER PRODUCTION ART

VARIOUS STH 225 COVER CONCEPTS BY TRACY YARDLEY!

NEAR FINAL VARIANT COVER FOR STH 225

SONIC #230 COVER CONCEPTS BY BEN BATES

SILVER SONIC III CONCEPT BY IAN FLYNN

SILVER SONIC I

› LARGE, IMPOSING, HULKING
› HEAVILY ARMORED
› SILVER & SHINY
› HUGE!!! x2 SONIC HEIGHT OR MORE

› WICKED SPINES!
› IGNORE LOGIC: BLADED BALL OF DOOM!

› RAZOR-BLADE SPINES
› SHINY! SILVER!
› ATTACHED IN SHEATHES

› BULKY ARMOR
› STILL STREAMLINED FOR SPEED

› FLATTENED FOREARMS FOR SHIELDS?

› ROCKET-PIPES WRAP AROUND LEGS

› WHEELS ON ANKLES WORK WITH ROCKET-PIPES

SILVER SONIC III

MECHA SALLY
BY BEN BATES

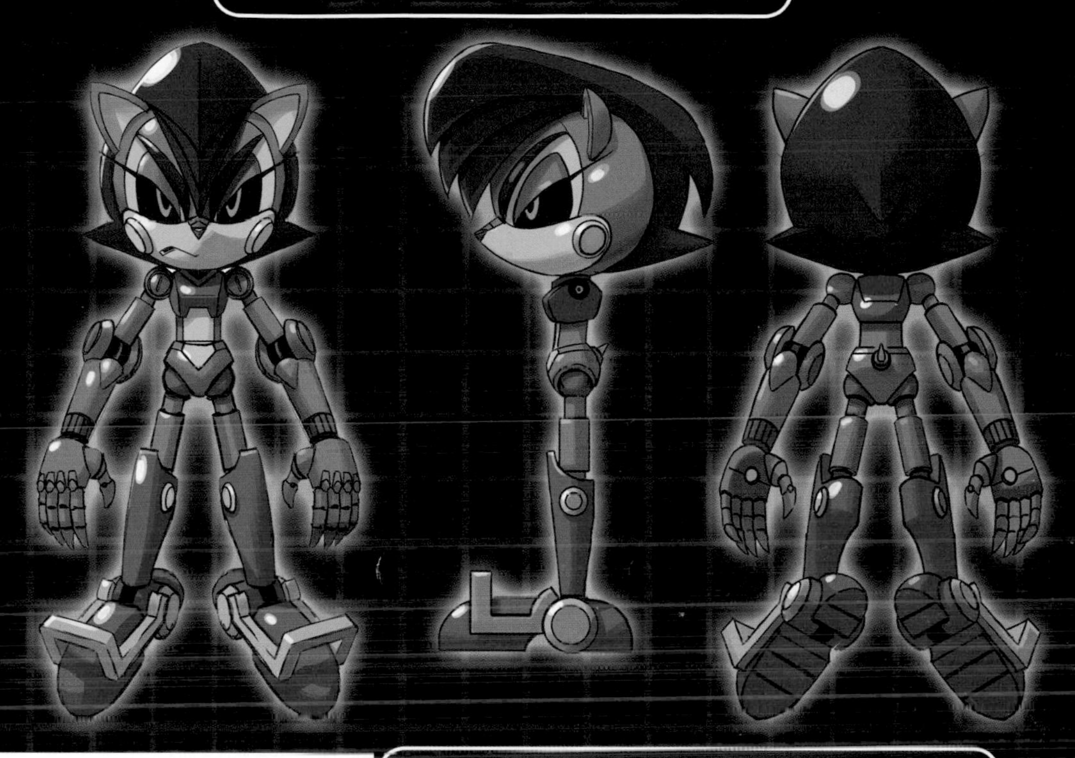

SONIC #229 COVER THUMBNAIL
BY PAUL KAMINSKI

SONIC THE HEDGEHOG

S/H #229 COVER

white

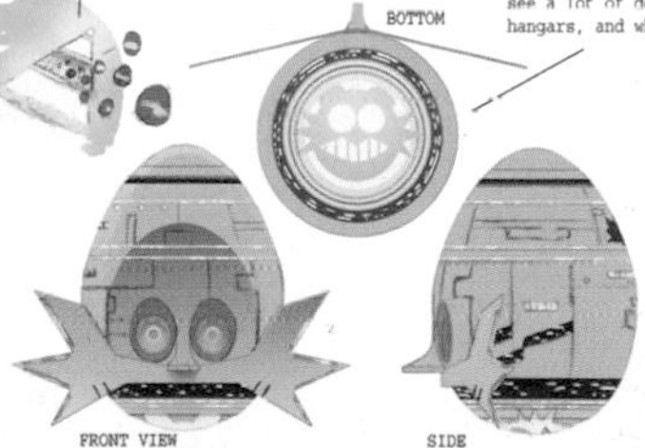

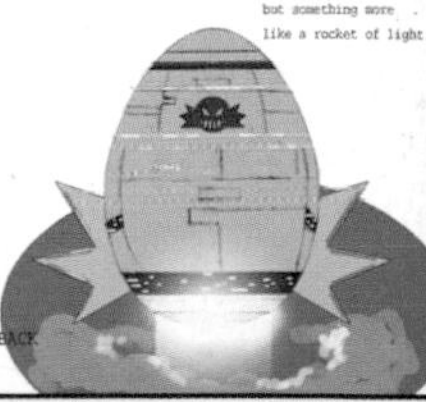

DEATH EGG II CONCEPTS BY BEN BATES